T H E S

The

Royal Maccabees Rocky Mountain Salvation Company

How The West Was Conned

A Novel by

R O N C A R T E R

Bookcraft
Salt Lake City, Utah

Apart from historical figures,
all characters in this book are fictitious,
and any resemblance to actual persons,
living or dead, is purely coincidental.

Library of Congress Catalog Card Number 98-74340
ISBN 1-57008-581-1

First Printing, 1998

Printed in the United States of America

"Cannonballs!" Timothy McPherson Doyle exclaimed under his breath. "Those gold nuggets are big as cannonballs! Bigger! Maybe twelve, fifteen pounds each."

He stared through the open double doors at one end of the ancient, slab-sided, dilapidated old livery barn next to the railroad station, mesmerized by the gleam of the gold that sparkled in a small shaft of June sunlight shining through a ragged hole in the old roof.

Beautiful, lovely, exquisite, enchanting, captivating, beguiling yellow gold! They were in chunks so big a man could hardly lift one without using both hands. He wiped at his mouth as he stared.

"Some of those are going to be mine," he promised himself.

He narrowed his eyes, squinting from the bright sunshine, and peered into the shadows inside the barn at the six men gathered at the back of a wagon hooked up to two large mules. The big double doors at the far end of the barn hung open on crooked hinges, and silhouetted two fat, fifty-five gallon wooden barrels on the hard dirt floor, near the rear of the heavy wagon. Even in the shadowy barn, Doyle could see a gigantic gold nugget plunked down on each barrel head. The wagon tail gate was down, ready to be loaded.

"Four of those guys are Indians," Doyle muttered.

He paused to reflect, then glanced left at the squat, mustard-colored building with POCATELLO IDAHO U.P. TRAIN STATION stencilled on the white sign. A railroad crew raised the dripping water tower arm, and cinched the cap back onto the water intake port on top of the black engine on the tracks, and waved to the engineer. Steam clouds billowed and hissed as the engineer released the clutch, and the two great drive shafts leaned into the weight of eighty-three loaded cattle cars. The drive wheels slipped on the worn, shiny tracks, the shafts whirred, then the drive wheels took traction and the cattle train crept slowly forward.

Doyle glanced nervously at the busy railroad crew to be certain no one had noticed him roll off the rods beneath the eighth cattle car as the train pulled into the station. A big man wearing a cap with UNION PACIFIC RAILROAD DETECTIVE printed on it eyed him suspiciously from sixty feet away. Doyle quickly brushed at the dried green-brown flecks on his black frock coat, and dusted his hat with his coat sleeve. He smiled benignly at the detective before he hurried down the hot, dusty street at the side of the livery barn, away from the railroad station.

He slowed, waited a minute to be sure he wasn't followed, and then he quickly, silently, dodged behind the side of the barn, beside a fly-infested pile of manure and decomposed straw from the stalls inside, and crouched beneath a grimy, broken window. The talk inside was low, mumbled, partly in Indian, partly in rich Irish, but two words Doyle understood only too well.

Whiskey.

Gold.

He took off his black Philadelphia gambler's hat and slowly, carefully, raised his head until he could see into the murky depths of the cavernous barn.

He gaped at the sight of the Indian standing nearest the barrels. The giant stood over seven feet tall, and weighed at least 400 pounds! A large leather pouch slung around his neck on a heavy leather strap bulged under his right arm. Beside him stood an average-sized Indian with a big hawk nose, doing the talking. On the other side was a smaller Indian with a dipper in his hand, a bucket on the floor at his feet, and a great smile on his face. Doyle smelled whiskey. Behind all of them was a diminutive Indian scarcely five feet tall with shifty eyes that missed nothing.

The hawk-nosed Indian was arguing in quiet, heated tones with the two white men. One wore a black bowler hat and a dirty white shirt closed at the throat, while the other wore buckskins, a big beard, and a battered felt hat over shoulder-length hair. The buckskin man had a knife and an old pistol holster on a belt around his middle.

"One nugget, one barrel," said the Indian.

Doyle squinted hard at the barrels, and suddenly swallowed hard. Scrawled on each barrel was the single word, "WHISKEY." His Irish ancestry would not be ignored, and he felt the grab in his stomach.

"Moonshiners!" Doyle whispered to himself.

The white man jabbed a pointed finger at the hawk-nosed Indian. "Naw, one barrel, two nuggets."

"Always before, one barrel, one nugget," insisted the Indian.

"Times is changed," the man with the white shirt argued. "These here is modern times. 1896! The gov'mnt has sent revenuers out here checkin' and it ain't like it used to be. We got a lot of risk. Two nuggets."

"You cheat. One nugget."

The white man shook his head violently. "Let's just fergit the whole deal. We'll take these here barrels on down the river and sell 'em to the Nez Perce Injuns. Chief Joseph'll give us gold and some of them funny colored horses. Them Nez Perce understands good whiskey."

"Chief Joseph no have gold nuggets this big. One nugget, one barrel."

It was true. No miner, no Indian, no settler, no government agent had ever seen gold nuggets to compare with those traded by the Blackfeet Indians who made their village just west of the Settlement. For generations, spies and thieves and government agents had invented every conceivable plan to discover where the gold came from, but none had succeeded. The source of the monstrous nuggets remained a mystery, and moonshiners came hundreds of miles to trade for them—one nugget, one barrel of whiskey—and the moonshiners grew wealthy.

"Nope, fergit it," the man in the bowler said. He turned to his companion in buckskin. "Roll 'em back into the straw stack and cover 'em. We'll load 'em after dark and barge 'em on down the river."

The bearded man seized the nearest barrel by the top rim and threw his weight against it to tilt it on its edge and roll it away.

"No take," the Indian said. He seized the nuggets from each barrel top and turned to the giant next to him. "Lump," he said.

The giant stepped forward, and the buckskin man reached for his pistol. The huge Indian seized his hand before the gun cleared leather. The buckskin man gasped and his face went white as the Indian squeezed the pistol free. The giant Indian grasped the pistol in both hands and effortlessly bent the pistol barrel back double and tossed the ruined gun into the wagon. Then the Indian gently lifted the motionless bearded man away from the whiskey barrel and set him down before he seized the barrel by the top and bottom and lifted it onto the back of the wagon.

Doyle's jaw fell open and quietly thumped on the windowsill. He watched the Indian casually lift the second barrel onto the back of the wagon.

"That ain't possible," Doyle whispered. "That gun barrel . . . no human alive can lift one of those fifty-five-gallon barrels filled with whiskey onto a wagon bed. Nobody!"

The talking Indian looked at the white men for a moment, then turned again to Lump and nodded. Lump took one step towards the bowler hat man, and the man quickly raised both hands defensively, with palms outstretched. His face was white and his voice was high and squeaky.

"One nugget, oh yeah, one nugget is just fine. I was only havin' some fun there for a minute. Musta got confused or somethin'. Just one nugget, like always. There ain't no risk, no gov'ment revenuers, no siree, one nugget will do just fine."

He stretched out his hands and the talking Indian plunked a fourteen-pound nugget into each of them.

"Thank you," the trembling man said. "Yessir, I hope you enjoy it. That's the best batch of white lightnin' we ever made. We got some more just as good comin' off 'fore fall, and we'll send word like always and we'll bring 'er on in like always, and we'll sell 'er for one nugget a barrel, just like always. Yessir, one nugget is just fine."

He doffed his bowler hat and smiled so hard his face nearly cracked as he bowed courteously to Lump. "Uh," he stammered, "Mr. Lump, you better be careful with the rest of them nuggets." He gestured toward the huge leather pouch. "There's lots of folks lookin' to get 'em. Yessir, Mr. Lump, you best be careful."

"Gold safe," the talking Indian said. "We go."

"Hey," rasped the buckskin man. "What about that pistol he ruint? Goldang it, he oughta pay fer it." He pointed at the mangled gun in one corner of the wagon bed.

The bowler hat man jabbed him in the ribs, then turned smiling to Lump. "Don't worry none about that pistol, Mr. Lump, no siree, we'll get another'n."

Lump hoisted the leather pouch clunking into the wagon beside the barrels, then lifted the tailgate with one hand and fastened it with the other. The talking Indian climbed into the wagon seat, Lump climbed up next to him and the seat sagged. The two smaller Indians scrambled into the back of the high-sided wagon and sat down beside the whiskey barrels, out of sight. The talking Indian gathered the reins to the sleepy-eyed mules and gigged them and yelled, "Giddap!"

The weathered, battered wagon squeaked and groaned into motion and rolled out the double doors from the gloom of the barn into open sunlight and turned right. It made broad tracks in the dusty, rutted Main Street of Pocatello, Idaho. Doyle trotted to the street, helplessly watching the rickety old wagon rumble eastward, past the unpainted, false-fronted stores of the railroad town.

His mouth became a straight line as he racked his brain, but he could not conceive of any way to stop it. He followed up the street behind it, mouth watering as he watched the two whiskey barrels through the dust. He passed the Chinese laundry, a saloon, Malloy's General Merc, Sven's Tonsorial Parlor, another saloon, a few more stores, an unpainted, steepled church, and the Bannock County Sheriff's Office. From the corner of his eye he saw the sheriff's door open. A paunchy, balding, bespectacled man with three day's growth of white whisker stubble and a high-topped beaver hat swayed out to the edge of the boardwalk. He waved a crumpled, yellow piece of paper in his right hand.

"Hold on there," he called to Doyle. "Leave off chasin' them Injuns and git on over here." He stepped into the dusty street and walked towards Doyle.

Doyle stopped and turned. A badge hung loosely on the sheriff's wrinkled, frayed white shirt, and a pistol handle peeked out of the right front pocket of his baggy trousers.

"You talking to me?" Doyle asked, eyes wide in wonder.

"Yeah, you," the sheriff growled. "I got this here telegram from Abe over at Corinne and he says watch out fer a dirty rotten skunk that swindled the Mormon bishop over there outta sixty bucks usin' marked cards in a poker game. Says this feller is about six feet tall and he's a charmer with black wavy hair and kin talk a bird out of a tree. That sounds a lot like you look, mister. Where you from?"

"Who's Abe, and where's Corinne, and what's a Mormon bishop doing playing poker in the first place?"

"Abe's sheriff in Corinne, and Corinne's in Utah, and the Mormon bishop thought he was playin' gin rummy. Now who are you, and when did you hit town?"

Doyle's mouth thinned, and he hunched forward to look up and down the street secretively to see if any of the local citizenry was within earshot, or watching. Two or three people were on the street, but they were a hundred yards distant, and talking together. Doyle walked close to the sheriff and thrust both his hands forward, wrists together, and leaned forward and whispered. "Put the cuffs on me. Arrest me. Take me in."

The sheriff's eyes bugged. "What? You crazy?"

"Don't ask no questions!" Doyle hissed. "Just slap the cuffs on and take me in. Throw me in jail."

"I ain't doin' no such thing," the sheriff said. "What kind of a crazy man asks to be arrested?"

Doyle dropped his hands and shook his head in disgust. "You won't arrest me?"

"No, at least not right now. Who are you?"

"Tim Doyle. I got in this morning."

The sheriff adjusted his iron-rimmed spectacles and inspected Doyle's black frock coat.

"Is all them brown specks what I think they are? You come in on the rods under a cattle car?" He pulled a wry face.

"Yeah, I did, and those brown specks is just what you think they are," Doyle replied. "Did Abe tell you whether that Mormon bishop got my suit-case?"

The sheriff bobbed his head. "He got it. Clothes, two decks of marked cards, a hunnerd and forty hard Yankee dollars, one bottle of Irish whiskey, and a badge from some marshall in Wyoming. How'd you git the badge? Shoot him?"

"No. He wanted to roll dice and didn't have money. I have to get that stuff. It's real important. Can you get it?"

"Git it yourself! How come you didn't bring the suitcase with you, if it was so all fired important?" The sheriff grinned. "Leave town in a hurry?"

Doyle looked perplexed. "I never seen nobody get a lynch mob so fast."

"The Mormon bishop?"

"No. His wife. Bishop cornered me in the hotel lobby while his missus was out about town and he insisted we play poker while I was waiting for the train. She walked in unexpected, he yelled cheat and pointed at me, and she stomped out the door hollering, and in twenty seconds, here come this mob with axe handles and forty feet of rope."

"The Mormon elders?"

"Elders nothing! The Mormon Relief Society. Women!"

"They got you?"

"No sir, I left my suitcase right there and I hit the railroad station two jumps ahead of that mob. That guy's wife must have weighed 240 pounds and I never seen a woman that size move so fast in my life. The cattle train was leaving and I swung under a car just as it was gathering speed. She couldn't get to the rods in time to jerk me out, but she whacked me a couple times with an axe handle."

"You owe that bishop sixty dollars?"

"Yeah. Tell him he can take it out of the one-forty in the suitcase, plus ten bucks for his trouble, if he'll send the rest of the money and the other stuff to me here."

"We'll see about that. Abe says he got a telegram from the marshall in Wyoming about that badge. You got some loaded dice with them marked cards?"

"He's worried about the badge? I'll send it back. Abe got a warrant out for me?"

The sheriff shrugged. "No, but that ain't the point anyway. The point is we don't want no tin-horns with marked cards and loaded dice in this town. You get right back on the next train goin' either direction, and don't come back."

Doyle glanced at the group of people still talking and leaned slightly forward to speak confidentially.

"I can't do that, sheriff." He glanced up the street again, face serious. He whispered, "I got a job to do here. Big. Won't take but a few days, and then I'll be gone."

"You figgerin' to knock off the bank?" The sheriff fondled the handle of his pistol.

Doyle looked disgusted. "No. A government job. Undercover. Big! Real big! I can't tell you more than that right now, but I can in a day or two, after I get through at the telegraph office. Is Dan Buttums still running the telegraph office?"

The sheriff scratched his ample jowls. "Nope, Josh Splivings. Don't recollect no Dan Buttums hereabouts."

Doyle shook his head sadly. "Them guys in Washington was wrong again. They told me Dan Buttums. Where's the telegraph office?"

The sheriff pointed. "Up past the train station on the north side of the street. Why're you so all fired intent on gettin' yerself arrested?"

"Cover. It'd help my cover."

"Cover fer what?"

"Can't say. That business in Wyoming, and in Corinne? That was to help my cover."

The sheriff cocked a suspicious eye. "Now looka here, Doyle. All this high-an'-mighty talk about makin' cover fer a government job and sendin' telegrams—you can do all you want, but not in this town. You keep movin'."

"Not before I finish my assignment." He thrust

his hands forward again. "If that isn't good enough, cuff me and haul me in."

The sheriff snatched his hat from his head and stomped his foot. "Now goldang it, I ain't goin' to arrest you. That'd cost a buck and two bits fer yer meals and a laundry bill fer the blankets, and I ain't goin' to do it. You just git back on to the train station and get outta town. There's a freight leavin' at 6:40 headed east, right back to Corinne. You be on it."

Doyle slowly shook his head, jaw set, determined. "No sir, I cannot do that. The U. S. government is depending on me."

The sheriff's neck puffed and his face reddened. "What I'll do, I'll get Walt and Billy and Posey, and we'll hawgtie you and shove you right back on the rods under a cattle car on that 6:40, and you kin collect a bunch more of them brown specks that fall through the gaps in the floorboards of them cattle cars while you think things over. That's what'll happen if you don't clear outta town!" The sheriff bobbed his head in finality.

"I'll just turn around and come right back," Doyle said firmly.

The sheriff threw his hat in the dust. "If you ain't the contrariest tinhorn I ever seen! Out here sassin' the sheriff, refusin' to leave town!"

Doyle softened. "I don't mean to cause you grief," he said.

"Grief! I ain't never hit nothin' like this before. Here I'm tryin' to run you outta town like I'm supposed to, and I used all the threats I know of, and you're just standin' there sayin' 'throw me in jail,' and I ain't goin' to do it, and you're beatin' up on me somethin' awful with this here American government thing, and I just ain't sure what I'm supposed to do next. Why can't you be a respectable tinhorn and be scared of jail, and git outta town when I threaten you?" The sheriff looked crestfallen.

Doyle shook his head sympathetically and dropped a warm and friendly arm around the sheriff's shoulder.

"Don't take it so hard. Tell you what I'll do. I'll check in with you every morning and evening until I'm finished here. It won't take more'n a couple days. I won't play cards or roll dice with anyone. I'll do my assignment so no one even knows what's going on, and in my final report to Washington, D.C., I'll tell them you were my main help. What name do I use in my report?"

The sheriff brightened. "Pat. Pat Gompers."

"Pat," Doyle said, "it's going to be all right. Just take care of Pocatello, and I'll do my job, and Washington, D.C. will probably name a holiday after you."

"What?" Pat's eyes popped wide.

"Gompers' Day. In memory of your silent help."

"Yeah," Pat breathed quietly. "Yeah. That'll sound good for re-election."

"You'll be re-elected for sure. And then, maybe governor."

Pat stopped stone-cold. "Gompers for Governor. I shoulda thought of that."

"One thing, Pat," Doyle said, arm still draped around Pat's shoulder. "I got to keep my cover for the next couple days. If anyone comes asking, tell them you've got me under secret surveillance. You'll arrest me when you've found out who the big leaders are."

"Yeah, okay."

Doyle dropped his arm and straightened. "Now, where can I get some new clothes, a bath and a shave?"

"Start right there at Malloy's fer the clothes, and then on over to Sven's Tonsorial. The hotel has baths."

"Much obliged. Remember. Surveillance. We're waiting for the big fish."

"Yeah," Pat said, grinning.

Doyle nodded his goodbye and started towards Malloy's.

Pat exhaled a great breath and stood in the street with his fingers hooked in his suspenders, feeling grand. *Gompers for Governor.* There was something about the sound of it.

Doyle strode purposefully back up the street towards the unpainted, weather-grayed building with the faded sign, MALLOY'S GENERAL MERC. KEVIN MALLOY, PROP. The sound of tense voices between the hotel and Sven's Tonsorial Parlor slowed him, and he stopped to look.

Half a dozen men from a railroad gang and four or five miners had a small man backed against the hotel wall. He was sitting in the dust, arms thrown over his head, canvas shirt and baggy pantaloons covered with street dirt. A three foot pigtail dangled from the topknot at the back of his shaved head, and the mob was jeering with curses and raucous laughter. Doyle set his jaw and swallowed hard before he pushed on through the door into Malloy's.

The smell of smoked meat, new clothing stacked on shelves, and an open pickle barrel washed over him and for a moment he stopped to savor it. He walked to the counter with the scales and the cash register and was reaching to tap the bell when the pleasant, lilting voice of a girl stopped him.

"Top of the mornin', sir. Can I help you?" The voice came from shelves stacked with dry goods and Doyle turned to look.

She was nineteen. Her eyes were blue and her hair was long and held back by a piece of red ribbon, and a wisp of black hair curled on her forehead. Her nose was straight and turned up, her mouth was generous and smiling. She stood four inches shorter than Doyle, but she walked firm and strong. Doyle saw shamrocks and smelled daffodils and bluebells nodding in fresh green fields.

"Top of the mornin' back to you, ma'am." He swept his hat from his head and a lock of his own black, curly hair tumbled to his forehead.

The girl stopped demurely in front of him, head cocked, smiling, eyes dancing. "Is there something I can help you with?"

"Pat said you might have some men's clothes."

"So it's clothes you'll be wanting?" the girl asked.

"Trousers and shirt, and a coat, and maybe a black hat. And a Bible. A big Bible."

"A Bible is it now? You're a man of the cloth?"

"Not exactly. I just need a big Bible."

"Fine. We'll start with the clothes." She led Doyle to some stacks on a shelf. "Your sizes should be right here."

A thin, elderly man with gray hair entered the front of the store. The girl smiled at Doyle again. "Reverend Gorten just came in for a special order," she said. "I'll be right at the counter. Call if you need help." She walked to greet the reverend.

Doyle picked out black cotton trousers, a fresh white shirt, a long tailed, black frock coat, a black ribbon necktie, and black socks. He tucked them under his arm, picked a black, wide brimmed, low crowned felt hat, and walked back to the counter. He laid the clothes beside a long roll of brown wrapping paper hung on a paper cutter.

"How much?"

The girl quickly sorted through the stack and ran a mental tally. "Thirteen dollars."

"A Bible?"

"Oh. Let me look." She disappeared through a curtain at the rear of the store.

The reverend brightened. "Did I hear someone mention the Bible?"

"That was me," Doyle said.

"You're a minister?"

"No."

"I'm Reverend Cuthbert Gorten of the church here in town. Non-denominational. I'd like to invite you to attend. Sunday mornings at ten."

"Thanks. I'll be there if I'm in town," Doyle said.

"You say you'll be down?" The reverend cocked his head forward and squinted an eye while he strained to hear.

"I said, if I'm in town."

"Wonderful. You'll be down. Sunday at ten." The reverend smiled broadly.

The girl returned. "Had that a long time," she said and laid a large Bible on the counter. Her face clouded. "It would be nice if people bought more Bibles and less liquor and bullets," she said.

"Did someone mention liquor?" the reverend inquired, cocking his head forward again.

"I did, Reverend," the girl said loudly. "I said, people should never use liquor."

"People should never use liquor," the reverend said sadly. "You don't sell liquor, do you Miss Malloy?"

She shook her head. "No."

"Good." He turned to Doyle. "No liquor here. You be down at the church Sunday?"

Doyle nodded. The reverend said goodbye, and shuffled out. Doyle smiled after him, and turned back to Molly. "How much for the Bible?"

"Three dollars. That makes sixteen dollars in all."

Doyle fished a Mormon bishop twenty dollar gold piece from his pocket and clacked it onto the counter. The girl counted his change and reeled a long sheet of wrapping paper off the roll.

"Could you wrap the trousers and shirt separate? I'll take them with me now and pick up the rest later."

The girl nodded and sorted the clothing.

"Malloy around?" Doyle asked.

The girl continued working. "I'm Malloy."

Doyle's eyebrows arched. "Kevin Malloy?"

"Molly. Kevin was my father."

"Was?"

"Passed on four years ago."

Doyle watched her as she reached for the string. "Illness?"

"He threw a tinhorn gambler out of the store one afternoon and when he was closing up that night, someone shot him and robbed us. It was the tinhorn, but no one could ever prove it. I despise tinhorns."

Doyle swallowed and shook his head slowly. "I'm sorry, ma'am. Truly."

She finished the knot and broke the string. "Pay it no mind. If you're not a minister, what use do you have for a Bible, if I might ask?"

Doyle lowered his voice. "It's for a special project." He picked up the smaller package. "Would you know who runs the laundry?"

She looked at his speckled clothes and smiled. "Ping Fat and his daughter, Fan. Good people."

Doyle pushed the larger package to Molly, and she put it under the counter with his dusty, battered hat.

"The hotel has baths?" Doyle asked.

"Tub in the back room. Fifty cents. The rest of your things will be waiting when you come back."

"Thank you, ma'am." He nodded and smiled and walked out the door.

The bath was hot and the soap strong. The new clothes were stiff and creased. He walked from the hotel back into the bright, hot sunlight towards the laundry. The huddle of men were still beside the hotel, still threatening the small Chinese, who had bowed his head between his knees with his arms clasped overhead and huddled in a ball to avoid the threatened beating.

Doyle entered the canvas tent that said PING FAT LAUNDRY and dumped his load of dirty clothes on the counter. A small Chinese man came through a curtain and faced him.

"Wash clothes?" asked Ping Fat in a high voice. He looked at the brown specks on the coat and his squinty eyes opened wide and he broke into a high, raucous laugh.

"How you get specks? Cow fly?" He whacked

the counter with his diminutive fist and laughed so hard his face went red and he gasped for breath.

Doyle chuckled and waited for Ping Fat to wipe his eyes and quit wheezing. "Yeah, those cows were flying. I've got to have these finished by late this afternoon, dry and ironed and in a package ready to go. How much?"

The man turned his head and spewed a singsong of Chinese over his shoulder, and a girl hurried through the curtain to his side. Fan's face and shoulders were round and her black eyes were humble and downcast as she bowed at least six times to Doyle. Ping Fat pointed and Fan sorted through the clothes quickly and said something singsong back to him, bowed to Doyle, and disappeared.

"Fo clock two dolla," Ping Fat said.

"Four o'clock, two dollars?"

Ping Fat bobbed his head. "Ya."

"Good. I'll pick them up."

Doyle walked back into the street and paused when he heard Ping Fat talking loudly to Fan in Chinese. He heard "Cow fly" and then they both broke into uproarious laughter.

Doyle grinned and strode on down the street to the tonsorial parlor and sat down in the empty barber chair. The pear shaped, baldheaded barber shifted the stub of a cigar from one side of his mouth to the other, popped the big cloth, and clipped it around Doyle's neck.

"Howdy. I'm Sven. Shave?"

"And haircut."

The man's scissors snicked and his hand shears clicked until Doyle's hair was trimmed. Then the man opened a steaming, black iron kettle and gingerly hot-fingered a smoking towel in the air until it cooled enough to avoid outright burns, and draped it around Doyle's face, while Doyle flinched and sucked air against the heat. From the small hole where the towel opened around his nose and mouth, Doyle asked, "Did you see those Indians and the wagon a while ago?"

"Yeah."

"That one Indian. Four hundred pounds?"

"Yep."

"Biggest I ever saw. Know who they are?"

"Blackfeet. Big one's named Lump. His mind's busted. He's about five years old, in his head. Happiest man I ever saw."

"Didn't know you had Blackfeet nearby."

"Sixty miles north."

"Reservation?"

"No. Well, sort of. They just got together up there where nobody ever goes much and settled in. They mind their own business and don't bother no one. Come here every few months to get a couple barrels of white lightnin' when some moonshiner comes through. Seem happy to just sit up there and sip moonshine and talk with the settlers."

"Near a town?"

"Nope. A place called the Settlement because there ain't no town."

"How do they get a wagon in there?"

"There's a freight wagon trail up there. Starts east end of town, heads straight north."

Sven stopped. "You interested in them Injuns?"

"Naw. Just wondered where Goliath came from.

I thought moonshining to Indians was illegal."

"It is, but nobody around here pays that law no mind."

"Even the sheriff?"

Sven shrugged. "What for? Them Injuns freight that stuff home and nobody ever heard of 'em causin' any trouble from drinkin' it up there. They offer it to travellin' strangers, share it with anyone. Friendly bunch."

"How do they pay for it?"

Sven stopped. "Gold. You got an interest in them nuggets? Is that it?"

"What nuggets?"

"The way you asked, I figured you seen them nuggets. If you did, ferget it. Forty years people been tryin' to find out where they come from. Best kept secret this side of the Missouri."

Doyle fell silent while Sven lifted the hot towel, lathered him, and worked with his razor. Finished, Sven wiped Doyle clean with a fresh hot towel, parted his hair dead center and combed it back, and splashed rose water on his face.

Doyle inspected himself in the mirror, ran his hand over a smooth cheek, rubbed his fingers upward against the prickle on the back of his neck, and reached into his pocket.

"How much?"

"Three dollars."

Doyle counted out the coins.

"Uh, if it ain't pryin', what's yer name and what's yer business here in town?" Sven ventured.

"Doyle. Just looking around."

"Fer what?"

Doyle glanced toward the street cautiously. "Can't say."

Sven's face clouded. "You an outlaw? You after the bank?"

Doyle smiled. "Ask Pat."

"Gompers? The sheriff?"

Doyle winked and clumped back out onto the boardwalk, and stopped at the sound of a commotion by the hotel. The rabble had the little Chinese man by the arms and were dragging him out into the street. Doyle turned back to Sven.

"What's going on over there?"

"Not much. Them Chinese ran outta work when the Union Pacific finished the railroad, and they just do what they can to stay alive, like Ping Fat and Fan. That one over there ain't got no job, and Slade and them rowdies keep threatenin' to cut off his pigtail just to bedevil him. He thinks if his pigtail's gone he ain't goin' to heaven."

Doyle shook his head and walked off the boardwalk into the dusty street. He walked past the raucous horde, on to the cafe with DELMONICO'S printed on the cracked sign above the door. He ate steak and potatoes slowly, in deep concentration. Finished, he wiped his face on a napkin, paid, stuck a toothpick in his teeth, and walked out into the sunlight.

The mob had moved out into the street, near the horse watering trough. Doyle lounged back against the restaurant wall to pick his teeth while he watched what they were doing.

The leader of the gang was hunched over the water trough, his arm thrust in nearly to his shoulder, and for a moment Doyle puzzled at it. Then one bare foot thrust up from the water, then the other, and the feet kicked for a moment, before falling limp. The coarse, bearded man straightened and hauled the loose body of the diminutive Chinese upright, shaking the little man while the others roared with laughter. The soaked, bedraggled head raised slowly and the eyes opened while the half-drowned man stared at those around him, trying to understand where he was.

The big man spat tobacco juice and plunged the little body back into the water while the others cheered him on.

Doyle drew a deep breath, then turned and walked on down the street, the bright sunlight reflecting off the hard finish of his new white shirt. He passed the livery barn and the train station, and continued to the squat building with WESTERN UNION printed on a sign. He slowed, then walked past it and stopped at the maintenance shed behind the building, with the big double doors half open. He glanced around and waited quietly for half a minute. He heard nothing but the sound of wind in the streets. He quickly slipped through the doors and waited inside until his eyes adjusted to the dim shadows.

He brightened at the sight of a high sided wagon with broad wheels, reinforced axles, double springs, a canvas top, and the letters WESTERN UNION burned into the wood on both sides. He lifted the canvas curtain at the rear and peered inside at four large, cast-iron storage batteries, shovels, a huge tool box, and a gigantic spool of copper telegraph wire.

He peeked out the door to be certain no one was near, then walked back into the street, and around to the front of the building. He paused at the front door while he quickly studied the lock, then opened the door and stepped inside.

Bzzzzzzhumpf. Bzzzzzzhumpf.

Old Josh Splivings sat behind the counter, chin on his chest while his deep, rhythmic snoring moved his long, lanky frame in and out. He wore a green eyeshade over bushy, gray eyebrows and a craggy face, and black arm garters circled his white shirt sleeves. Doyle grinned and closed the door behind himself with a bang.

"Whazzat who dunnit!" exclaimed Josh as his head jerked up and he tried to focus his weary, watery blue eyes.

"Oh, pardon me," Doyle said affably. "Didn't know you was sleeping."

Josh blinked his eyes and his enormous Adam's apple bobbled as he cleared his throat and worked his mouth a time or two. He shifted in his chair and the floor creaked. "Wasn't sleepin'. Nossir. Just concentratin'. What can I do fer you?"

"I'm going to need to send a telegram sometime today or tomorrow. I need to know your rates."

Josh was still shaking his head, working with his eyes to get a clear focus. "Yessir. Rates. Wellsir, them rates is cal-clated by the word and the mile. Where is this here telegram going?"

"Washington, D.C. And maybe to Baltimore."

Josh shook his head and squinted to focus on Doyle. "You shore about that? That's . . . lemme get this here chart."

He fumbled through a book and ran a finger down a page.

"Why that's better'n three thousand miles. I ain't never sent no telegram that far before. Says here we got to send it two hours early. Don't say earlier'n what, just early. You shore about all this?"

"What are your hours?"

"Not hours. Sendin' a telegram don't take more'n five, ten minutes, not hours."

"What hours are you open?"

"Oh. Why didn't yuh say so in the first place? Eight of a mornin' til five of an afternoon. 'Cept noon. I get an hour at noon. I don't take no hour eatin', but what I do, I got this system worked out. I eat up at Delmonico's and then I come back here an' concentrate for the rest of the hour." Old Josh smiled at the clever arrangement.

"Did you find the rates?"

Josh studied the grid on the page, where the rates were across the top of the grid and the mileage along the left edge.

"Well," he said, and cocked an eye at Doyle, "the way they got this here thing worked out, it'll take a little time to figger it. Tell you what. You just come on in when you got yer telegram writ down the way you want 'er, and I'll give you a special deal. Yessir. I'll take the reg'lar rate to Denver, and we'll just double 'er. That oughta do it."

"That'll be fine," Doyle said. "Thanks for your time."

"Time's free," Josh said.

Doyle walked out and back to Malloy's store. Molly looked up from the counter, froze, and gaped.

Bathed, shaved, haircut, new trousers and shirt, Doyle stood before her a new man.

"It's fine you're lookin' in your new clothes. Have you come for your other package?"

Doyle blushed. "I have. And I thank you for holding it."

She put the package on the counter, and he opened it and took out the ribbon tie and the coat and socks. Molly pointed to the full-length mirror nailed to the wall at the rear of the store and Doyle walked back and tied his tie and slipped into his new socks and black frock coat. He walked back to her at the counter.

She handed him his Philadelphia gambler's hat, and he paused. It was carefully cleaned and brushed and looked nearly new. He glanced at her, startled.

"It never looked so good. When'd you do that?"

She smiled and blushed. "Just did it."

"What do I owe you?"

"Nothing."

"Could you wrap the new hat and the Bible back into that paper, to carry?"

He glanced around the room and located a clock while she tied the package. Nearly four o'clock. She pushed the package to him.

"I thank you." He gathered the package. "I surely do."

"You're welcome."

He smiled and walked out the door, and Molly Malloy walked to the window to watch him. He strode purposefully towards the laundry, past the crowd of men who were still abusing the little Chinese. They were dragging him up the street by a rope looped around his neck, headed for the livery barn.

Doyle's jaw clamped shut and for a moment small ridges appeared along his jawline. He slowed and held up his hand. He smiled at the leaders of the swarm and they stopped. The screen door to Sven's banged and from the corner of his eye Doyle saw Sven step onto the boardwalk. Behind him, he heard a firm, determined step and quickly looked to see Molly stride into the dusty street, fists clenched, eyes on fire. Four or five people pushed out of the cafe onto the boardwalk and stood to watch.

Molly stormed past Doyle and stopped directly in front of Slade, hands on her hips, feet spread.

"So it's tormentin' little folk, is it! Why you ought to be ashamed of yourself, the whole lot of you! He's done you no harm so you're going to do him no harm. You let him go this minute!"

Slade recoiled and blinked his eyes for a moment in startled amazement. Then a slow, insolent grin spread on his grimy face.

"Well if that don't beat all! I do believe we got us a genuine do-gooder here. I'll bet she don't hold with a man havin' a nip once in a while neither. How about it, ma'am?" He lifted his battered hat from his head. "Care to step into the saloon with us for a wee nip?"

Slade's men roared their approval, and Slade reached for her arm.

Molly jerked away from him. "Your habits are an abomination, and you're going to let that man go. Now. This minute."

The grin disappeared in Slade's tobacco-stained beard. "And if we don't?"

Molly shook her finger under his nose. "You will!"

The grin re-appeared. "Watch that finger, ma'am," Slade said, "it might be loaded. And I figger you better accept my invitation, and come on with us for a little nip, and to watch the hangin'."

Those behind him howled with glee.

Slade grasped her arm and Molly jerked but could not escape. Slade turned to pull her up the street with the mob.

Doyle pushed past through the mob and faced Slade. "Havin' a little fun?" he asked amiably.

The mob stopped and the Chinese dropped to his knees, his head tipped forward in quiet acceptance of his fate.

Slade's face turned ugly. "You with her? You goin' to try to save this here China heathen too?"

Doyle glanced around. "With who? Her?" He pointed at Molly. "Me? Never seen her before today. I'm just passin' through. Figured to watch the fun, if that's what you got in mind."

Slade looked suspicious for a moment, then the reckless grin returned. "Yeah," he said. "Ain't it a caution? We're goin' to have a drink, me and her, and then she's gonna help us in gettin' rid of this heathen."

"What's he done?"

"Nothin'. Heathen's was borned to get hung and we're headed to the livery barn where there's a rafter high enough to oblige this one." Their laughter rang.

Doyle laughed with them. "You know, that might be worth watchin', but I been thinking. I might could use a heathen to carry my baggage. Tell you what. I'll make you a deal you can't resist."

Slade released his hold on Molly, and she yanked her arm and stepped away from him. He held up his hand and the crowd fell silent, waiting.

Doyle cleared his throat. "Do you figure you would have more fun with a couple bottles of whiskey?" He pulled coins from his pocket.

Murmurs broke out.

"Naw, a hangin' would be more fun."

Doyle shrugged. "You're probably right. Okay, tell you what. We'll roll dice for him. You win, you get your drink with the lady, hang the Chinaman, and you get my money for two bottles of whiskey to boot. You lose, the lady goes free, I get the heathen, and you get my money for two bottles of whiskey anyway."

Slade scratched his ragged, dirty beard. "We get the whiskey either way?"

"Yep."

"You got a deal. Where's some dice?" He turned to the mob. Some searched their pockets, but each shook his head. They had no dice.

Doyle patted his pockets. "Seems to me I had . . . there they are. Sheriff over in Corinne gave me some dice a couple days ago—took them off some tinhorn. Told me to get rid of 'em but I forgot," Doyle said. He pulled his three dice from his pocket, one hidden between thumb and forefinger. "Let's get someplace and we'll roll 'em."

"Right here on the boardwalk," Slade said, and Doyle followed him. They gathered around and Doyle shook the dice in his hand and blew on them and shook them again while the men circled him and fell into silence, breathless.

He shook his hand again and, with a sweep of his arm, threw two of the dice rattling on the boards while he palmed the third one. The dice bounced off the front of the building and skittered back and settled.

"Seven," Doyle said, dejected. "I guess that means I lose."

"You got 'er backwards," Sven hollered from the crowd. "Seven wins!"

Doyle's jaw fell open and his eyes popped. "I win? With a seven?"

"Yep," Sven said. "Too bad, Slade," he called to the leader of the gang. "Doyle gets the Chinaman and Molly goes free."

There was grumbling from Slade's gang, and general murmuring among the others that had gathered to watch.

"Well, now," Doyle stammered, "I didn't really figure on . . . I don't know much about owning somebody."

Slade stepped directly in front of Doyle and his hand dropped to his knife handle. "Maybe you don't own nobody," he growled. "Let's see them dice. I reckon they're loaded."

Doyle's face went blank with affronted innocence. "Loaded! Loaded? You think those dice are loaded?"

"Hand 'em over," Slade demanded, and pulled his knife from its sheath and held it loosely at his side.

"Well, come to think of it, that might just be

true," Doyle stammered. "That sheriff took 'em off that tinhorn and tossed 'em to me. I never thought of that. How do you check to see if they're loaded?"

"Just give 'em to me," Slade snarled.

"Yes sir," Doyle said. He thrust his hand into his pocket and grasped all three dice, and dropped two of them into Slade's filthy, outstretched hand while he deftly palmed the third one.

Slade hefted them, first together, then separate. He rattled them together in his hand, then dropped to his knees in front of the boardwalk.

"Here's how you tell if they're loaded," he said. "You throw 'em, and if they come up seven again, we'll get our two bottles of whiskey and a double hangin'—you and the Chinaman both!"

Doyle sucked air and looked around frantically. "You mean you'd hang me if that sheriff gave me loaded dice?"

"We'd hang you for cheatin' us," Slade exclaimed.

He threw the dice against the wall of the building. They rattled and danced and came to rest.

Slade counted the spots. "Nine," he said with disgust.

"Does that mean they're loaded?" Doyle asked.

Slade gathered the dice and again he rattled them in his hand and cast them against the building. They clattered and came to rest.

"Five," Slade said and stood.

"Are they loaded?" Doyle asked again.

"It don't appear so," Slade said through gritted teeth, "but somehow you cheated us."

"How?" Doyle exclaimed, his shoulders

hunched, eyes wide and innocent. "You threw the dice."

"I dunno yet, but when I figger it out, you better be a far piece from here. Gimme the whiskey money."

"Oh, yeah," Doyle said, and dug two five dollar gold pieces out of his pocket. "That oughta buy two bottles of good whiskey."

Slade grabbed the coins and Doyle gathered his dice.

"Yeah," Slade said, "but when I figger out the dice deal, I'm comin' lookin' for you."

Doyle slowly straightened and stuffed the two dice in his pocket where they settled with the third one. He slowly brought his eyes to meet Slade's. Gone was Doyle's innocent look, his affable smile. His jaw was set, his dark eyes glittering like burning flecks of obsidian.

"Yeah, Slade," he said so quietly only Slade could hear. "You do that. When you figure it out, you come find me. We'll talk it over, you and me."

Slade looked into Doyle's eyes, caught his breath, and involuntarily took a step back. He licked his suddenly dry lips and he stammered, searching for words, but none would come.

The nasal twang of Pat Gomper's voice cut through the crowd. "Awright, now you just break up this here crowd. Git movin'. Git."

The crowd began to break up and Pat muscled his way to where Doyle stood facing Slade.

"Jist what do you think yer doin' this time?" Pat said to Slade. "You roughin' up that little fella? You'n that gang of riff-raff git on outta here."

Slade turned on his heel and walked back through his mob. "Come on," he muttered, "we got some serious drinkin' to do."

Pat waited a moment, then turned to Doyle. "You in the middle of that somehow?"

Doyle's eyes widened. "Me? No sir. I was just on my way to get some laundry."

Pat turned to Molly. "You see this thing?"

"Yes."

"This fella mixed up in the ruckus?"

Molly shook her head. "No. He was trying to break it up."

Pat looked at Doyle suspiciously. "You better get that gov'nment job finished and move on quick. Slade don't take to nobody messin'. Don't fergit about mentionin' me in that telegram to Washington. Gompers. Pat Gompers."

"Yes sir, like I told you, I'll be finished and gone in a couple of days. I won't forget—Sheriff Pat Gompers."

Pat walked away, while Molly waited beside Doyle.

"It was a good thing you did," she said. "I'm thankin' you."

Doyle shook his head. "Ma'am, you ought not make a habit of taking on a guy like Slade with only your finger."

Molly cocked her head and arched one eyebrow. "How did you know you could roll that seven? Are those dice loaded?"

Doyle pursed his mouth for a moment. "That seven saved a lot of grief. Best not look too hard at it."

"It's as I thought," Molly said, "the dice *are* loaded. What did Pat mean, a telegram to Washington and mention his name?"

Doyle quickly raised his finger to his lips and shushed Molly. He looked around to see who might have heard. "Don't say anything about that."

"Are you an undercover government agent?"

Doyle frowned. "Ma'am, I'm tellin' you, don't say that out loud. If that reached the wrong ears . . ." He trailed the sentence off and stared at Molly with horror in his eyes.

Molly looked around and then leaned forward. "I won't repeat it. Are you?"

Doyle's face sobered. "Can't say."

Molly gasped. "You are!"

Doyle shook his head.

The little Chinaman, still on his knees waiting for his fate, looked up imploringly at Doyle, and touched his trouser leg. Molly composed herself and looked down at him.

"I doubt he understands what has happened."

Doyle helped him to his feet, and gently lifted the rope from his neck and tossed it into the street.

"You speak English?" Doyle asked. "What's your name?"

The man looked up into his face and smiled weakly.

"It is as I thought," Molly said. "He doesn't understand."

Doyle took him by the arm. "I'll take him to the laundry. Maybe Ping Fat and Fan can help."

"I'll be going with you, if you don't mind," Molly said.

"What about the store?"

Molly shrugged. "Customers will help themselves and leave the money on the counter. I won't be long."

They walked the little man to the laundry and pushed through the tent flap door. Doyle's finished laundry was on the counter, wrapped in brown paper. Ping Fat looked at Doyle, then Molly, and then stared at the disheveled little Chinese man, then back at Doyle.

"Two dolla," Ping Fat finally said, and Doyle plunked two dollars on the counter and took his package.

"Mr. Ping Fat," he said, "that bunch at the saloon was going to hang this man, and they might still try it. Would you hide him and get him on a train out of town? I'll pay for his ticket."

Ping Fat looked at Molly's serious eyes and hesitated for a moment. Then he spoke over his shoulder and Fan quickly slipped through the curtain and came around the counter. She looked at the small man, standing with his head bowed, dirty, his pigtail dangling, and she shook her head. There was pain in her eyes as she gently took hold of his arm, and led him back through the curtain.

Doyle laid a ten dollar gold piece on the counter. "Buy him a ticket somewhere he'll be safe," he said.

Ping Fat shook his head. "No pay. I take care." He bobbed his head several times.

"You sure?" Doyle asked.

Ping Fat bobbed his head vigorously.

Molly reached to cover Ping Fat's small hand

with hers. “Thank you,” she said, and Ping Fat bowed slightly.

Doyle picked up his ten dollars and walked out the tent flap with his package under his arm. Molly followed and caught up with him.

“Mr. Doyle,” she said, matching him stride for sturdy stride, “you might as well tell me why you’re here. I’ll get it out of Pat if you don’t.”

Doyle shook his head. “There’s nothing in the world so persistent as the curiosity of a woman,” he said with resignation. “I’m telling you, ma’am, you better leave well enough alone. You mix into this and there will be bad trouble. Maybe a war.”

Molly clapped her hand over her mouth. “A war?”

Doyle nodded slowly. “A war. Leave it alone.”

“A war with who?”

He did not slow, nor did he look at her or speak.

“You’ve got to tell me,” she insisted.

Doyle marched steadily up the street. “You’ll have to excuse me, ma’am. I’ve got to get registered at the hotel, and then I’ve got some messages to write, and I have to see Pat tonight.”

“Secret messages! With Pat!”

Doyle held his stride. “You better get back to the store. Forget all this.”

He suddenly turned toward the hotel and left her standing in the street. She watched him enter the hotel, and a few moments later she made her way to the store, looking back at the hotel, her face a study in insatiable curiosity.

Doyle stopped inside the hotel lobby and watched as Molly finally walked to the store and disappeared inside. He turned to the bald-headed desk clerk.

"I'll need a room for a night or two."

"One dollar a night. Sign here." He pointed to the register and turned to pick a key from a box. "Room 205, second floor, end of the hall. Uh . . . be careful about the sheets. They was fresh this mornin' and we don't change but once a week."

Doyle marched up the stairs into the room. He put his package of laundered clothes on the closet shelf, hung his coat on a hanger, and laid stretched out on the bed, hands behind his head while he pondered the next few days.

At 6:30 he counted his money, put on his coat, and went to Delmonico's for supper. At 7:30 he walked down the main street, in gathering shadows, and stopped at the darkened door of the sheriff's office. He cupped his hands about his eyes to peer closely through the glass door. There was light coming from beneath the rear office door.

Doyle rattled the handle, then knocked loudly. He waited, then banged again, and the door at the rear of the office opened. A lamp hung over a table, and Doyle saw stacks of poker chips, two whiskey bottles, and figures lurking in the heavy cigar smoke. Pat Gompers peered at him, then clumped through the office and opened the door.

"What's so goldanged important this time of evenin'?" Pat growled.

"Nothing. I was supposed to report to you each morning and evening until I'm out of town. I'm reporting. Things are okay."

"You've reported. Now git."

"Yessir. Uh . . . do I see a poker game back there?"

"Shore you see a poker game."

"Isn't gambling illegal in this town?"

"Not as long as the law is there, supervisin'. I'm there supervisin'."

"That stack of chips yours? And that extra hand at the empty seat?"

"Shore they are. That's how you supervise."

"Oh. Is that game open or closed?"

Pat scrutinized Doyle with a jaundiced eye. "Why? You want in?"

"I'm not much at poker."

"Cost that Mormon bishop sixty hard Yankee dollars to find out how much you ain't at poker. That game is closed to you."

"Oh," Doyle said. "Well, can't blame me for trying. See you tomorrow morning."

Pat glanced back at the poker table and the whiskey bottles for a moment, and scratched his whiskered jaw. "Naw," he said, "fergit about reportin' in the mornin'. I'll look you up about noon."

Doyle shrugged and stepped off the boardwalk in deep, late evening shadows. Pat closed the door and in a moment the window in the sheriff's door darkened. Doyle glanced up at a three-quarters waxing moon. It cast a silvery pallor that hid the dullness of the dusty street and the slab-sided, unpainted buildings, and created a sort of rustic beauty all around. The air was warm and still, and nighthawks wheeled and darted overhead.

He glanced at the laundry, where the back

portion of the long tent glowed with lamp light, and Doyle wondered when Ping Fat would get the small, abused man on the train. He thrust his hands in his pockets and, caught up in the silvery peace, walked slowly on toward the hotel.

The movement and the hiss came at the same time and Doyle recoiled and spun, braced, balanced, ready.

"Show yourself," he commanded.

"It's me," came the voice again, and a shadowy figure moved from the darkness and approached him quickly.

Doyle exhaled held breath. "Ma'am, I ain't armed, but folks been shot dead for doin' what you just done."

"I'm sorry, truly, but I saw you leave Pat's office a few minutes ago. Who are you? Why are you here?"

Doyle stood still in the moonlight and stared down at the large, dark eyes and cameo face framed by the long, black hair. He felt a stirring and for a moment remained silent.

"I can't tell you, ma'am."

"Molly. Call me Molly."

"Molly, I'll be gone in a day or two and it won't bother you any more."

"It will! I have to know," she said intently.

For long seconds he stood staring at her, lost in the deep pools of her blue eyes, while she stared back. Finally he shook his head.

"Good night."

He turned and walked quickly to the hotel.

"Mr. Doyle!"

Doyle stopped and turned as Molly strode hastily across the street in the bright, warm, clear mid-morning sunshine.

"Fan came to find me earlier. The man you saved—his name is Wong—doesn't want to leave town. He wants to stay with you and be your helper."

Doyle gulped and his head jerked back. "No way is he going with me!"

"Please go see him. He's so afraid. He says no matter where he goes, white people scorn him. You're the first white man that ever did anything kindly to him."

"Well I guess I learned my lesson!" Doyle exclaimed.

"Kindness is never wrong," Molly said, her eyes pleading. "Go talk to him. You'll see."

"I'm headed out of town and things are apt to get lively where I'm going. I can't even talk to him. It's too dangerous. There's no way he's going with me and that's final."

Molly stopped and tipped her head back to look directly into Doyle's eyes, and for long seconds she held his gaze. "Please," she said softly.

Doyle squinted one eye in exasperation, and moved his feet. "I can't take him."

Molly didn't move. Her eyes bored into Doyle's. "Please."

Doyle shook his head and raised his hands, palms outward. "Molly, you cut that out. Using your feminine wiles in an argument like this isn't fair."

"I'll go with you to talk to him."

"No."

"Then you go alone. Promise."

"I won't promise anything."

"Promise me."

Doyle jerked his hat off his head and pounded it on his thigh. "There's no way I can take him, don't you understand? I'll get him hurt. I'll get him killed. I can't talk to him. I can't warn him. I can't do anything with him. Can't you see that?"

Tears formed in Molly's eyes. "Please?"

Doyle clapped his hat back on his head and reddened with rage. "Yeah, okay, I'll go talk to him!"

Molly's face glowed, her eyes clear, and she smiled. "Thank you."

"Oh, you are ever welcome." He spun on his heel and nearly ran up the street while Molly smiled demurely and walked back to the store.

Doyle marched into the laundry tent and pounded on the counter. Ping Fat charged through the curtain with a shotgun in his hands, eyes wildly looking past Doyle for the hoodlums threatening to knock the place to pieces.

"Where robbers, where robbers?" he shouted at Doyle while he eared back both hammers of the shotgun.

The sight of the diminutive man waving a cocked shotgun sobered Doyle. "Whoa there, hang on. It's just me. I rapped too hard. Put that thing down."

Ping Fat lowered the shotgun and eased the hammers down. "What you want?"

"Is Wong here?"

Ping Fat spoke and Fan led Wong through the curtain, holding onto his arm and smiling at him reassuringly.

"Is he okay now?" Doyle asked Ping Fat.

"He plenty okay. No leave. Stay with you. Plenty okay."

Doyle shook his head vigorously. "Not plenty okay. I leave town soon. Go bad places. Wong can't go with me."

Ping Fat spoke to Wong. Wong answered, his face lighted and he smiled so broadly his eyes nearly closed. Ping Fat turned to Doyle. "Wong say he go with you. Don't care where. Don't care get hurt. He go with you."

"He can't! I'll get him killed! Don't you understand?"

Ping Fat showed all his teeth with his monster grin. "Understand plenty good. He go with you. Be ready any time."

Doyle threw up his hands. "This town is crazy!"

Fan stepped forward, bowed to Doyle, and held her eyes on the floor while she spoke.

"Wong fine man, good help. Trust you, no one else. Be your servant, helper. No care where you go, what go wrong. Please take Wong with you."

Doyle turned on his heel and planted his feet

and clenched his fists for a moment then turned back. "I bet you and Molly planned this whole thing. Women don't play fair. Okay. I'll think it over."

Ping Fat grinned. "Say when, he ready to go."

"Yeah, I'll tell you when." Doyle walked out into the bright sunlight shaking his head, muttering about women and reason and that in the eternal scheme of things the two would remain strangers forever.

"Hold on there!" a deep voice boomed.

Doyle turned to watch Slade and two of his mob come trotting from the saloon. Slade stopped a scant four feet from Doyle, his hand on his knife.

"I figgered it out. You had three dice an' that's how you cheated us. Let me see them dice." The men with him cursed and shook their fists.

Doyle took a deep breath and spoke quietly. "Slade, I had a bad night, and a bad morning, and I don't recall ever being in a worse mood. You're right. I had three dice. Two were loaded. I cheated you. But that ain't all." Doyle cleared his throat and continued. "My aunt Polly had the oldest, flea-bittenest, beat-upest, ugliest mule I ever saw, but along side you, old Sadie was a beauty. I don't have no idea how God made anything as ugly as you, or that smelt worse, or needed killing more." He unbuttoned his coat and slipped his right hand inside. "And considering the mood I'm in, I just might be able to hold back from dropping you right where you stand, if you'll shut your ugly mouth and take that buffalo face of yours somewhere else until things get a little better for me. You've got ten seconds to get going."

Slade gasped and reared back and jerked out his knife. "You threatnin' me?" he blurted.

"No, Slade, I'm just stating the facts. You've got eight seconds left before I pull out this Derringer and put a .41-caliber ball right between the two ugliest eyes this side of a pig."

"Why you . . ." Slade blustered. "I oughta carve out your gizzard right here and now." He raised his knife.

"Yes sir, if I was you that's exactly what I would do. Five seconds."

"You ain't got no Derringer in there. You're bluffin', just like them dice."

"Right again, Slade. I'm bluffing. I don't have a Derringer. You should step right over here and carve me up real good. Three seconds."

"I got friends here who'll git you if you git me."

"Yeah, you've got two friends, and this Derringer is only a double-barrel, which means one of your friends might live. But that won't mean much to you because the first shot takes out the middle of the one eyebrow you've got. Slade, either make your move or shut up and get outta here. I'm sick of talking to you."

"You got no right . . ."

"No right at all. One second."

Doyle jerked his hand up. Slade turned on his heel and hurried towards the saloon without looking back—storming and muttering the whole way—with his cohorts right behind.

Doyle waited until Slade passed through the swinging doors before he lowered his hand and started on towards the cafe.

"You in trouble again?" The twangy voice stopped Doyle, and Pat came waddling from his office door.

"No, I'm not."

"The way Slade pulled out that knife and cussed, I figured you was gonna git carved."

Doyle shrugged. "Changed his mind, I guess."

Pat looked at him with one eyebrow raised. "You packin' iron? I'm gonna have to take a look."

Doyle opened his coat to show there was no weapon. "Satisfied?"

"Got a Derringer up your sleeve?"

"No. Want me to take off the coat?"

"Naw, won't be necessary. When you leavin' town?"

"Probably tomorrow."

"See to it."

"I will. Who won the poker game you was 'supervising' last night?"

Pat grinned. "Walt," he sniggered. "I lost, but I got my commission for supervisin'."

"Ten percent?"

"Ten!" Pat looked insulted. "You don't know nothin' about supervisin'. Twenty."

"Not bad. That game over?"

"That game ain't never over," Pat exclaimed.

"Well, I've got things to do. I'll check in with you this evening."

Pat considered for a minute. "Yeah, well, if the lights ain't on in the office part, don't bother."

"You going to be supervisin' again tonight?"

"Yep. Most every night. Keeps me in pocket money, win or lose."

"Right." Doyle said good-bye and and walked on to Delmonico's and settled into a table near the front door. He read the menu and paid for coffee and a piece of Ruby's genuine fresh peach pie. He slowly ate his pie and sipped at the coffee and waited.

At 12:06 P.M. Josh clumped across the boardwalk and pushed through the door and settled at a small table near the window.

"Howdy, Ruby," he called to the woman standing at the counter. "Bring the usual."

Ruby smiled tiredly and moved her 220 pounds into the kitchen. She dipped mashed potatoes and gravy, slapped a pork chop onto a plate, and reached for the coffee pot.

Doyle quickly slipped out into the street. He glanced both ways, then strode briskly up to the Western Union office. The door was locked.

He drew a small, steel wire from his coat lapel and worked with it swiftly in the lock. Within five seconds the door was open and he stepped inside. Behind the counter, he opened the drawers of the desk in rapid succession until he found envelopes and stationery with the Western Union seal. He folded half a dozen sheets of the stationery around three envelopes and slipped them inside his breast pocket.

Next, he opened the TELEGRAPHER'S GUIDE on Josh's desk and flipped to the chart and maps of time zones, and the list of sending and receiving times. He carefully checked Washington, D.C., and Baltimore, made a mental note, and closed the book. The last thing he did was check the registration on the base of the telegraph key. It was registered to Joshua Ebenezer Splivings. Doyle returned to the door, checked to be certain everything looked as it had when he entered, set the lock, closed the door, then sauntered back into the street.

He walked over to the train station and slumped onto the rough cut pine bench and lounged back, feet kicked forward, and watched and waited. Ten minutes later Josh ambled up the street, opened the Western Union office door with his key, and walked in. Doyle watched the door for a few minutes before he stood, stretched, and walked back to the hotel.

In the lobby, he settled onto a chair at the desk by the window, and reached for the ink pen. He drew the Western Union stationery from his pocket. Half an hour later, he carefully folded two sheets of paper, inserted them in separate envelopes, and sealed them. With a flourish and swirl, he wrote the name "Joshua Ebenezer Splivings" on the outside of each envelope followed by "Utmost Confidential."

He put the remaining stationery back into his pocket, followed by the sealed envelopes, then rose, yawned, and walked up to his room.

At 4:40 P.M. he left the hotel and walked rapidly to the Western Union office and entered.

Bzzzhumpff. Bzzzhumpff.

Doyle shook his head. "Josh, you concentrating again?"

"Whazzat?"

"Wake up. We have important business."

"Just concentratin'. See, I got this system . . ."

Doyle cut him off. "I know all about your system. I need you wide-awake. We've got the most important business you'll ever handle. Are you awake yet?"

Josh worked to focus his eyes. "Yeah, sure. What's so all fired important?"

"First, check the back room while I look outside. No one, absolutely no one, can hear this."

Josh's eyes widened. "What're you talkin' about?"

"Just check the back room. I'll be right back."

Doyle walked out the front door, circled the building and the maintenance shed, and walked back in.

"Nobody outside. Okay inside?"

"Ain't nobody here but us."

"Okay. Josh, sit down. This isn't going to be easy."

"Now hold on here," Josh fumed. "Why am I sittin' down?"

"To keep from falling down. Now listen."

Doyle looked out into the street one more time, then leaned forward on the counter, close to Josh.

"My name is Jeremiah Pinkerton. I am . . ."

Josh gasped. "You're a Pinkerton man?"

Doyle grimaced. "Not so loud. Don't say that name again. You could provoke terrible trouble."

He waited for Josh to settle down and started again. "I'm Jeremiah Pinkerton, and I'm here on special assignment. Did you get the coded telegram from Washington, D.C.?"

Josh's jaw dropped onto his chin. "What telegram?"

Doyle's eyes rolled back into his head. "It should have been here yesterday afternoon—3:30 their time. Didn't you get it?"

"No such thing!"

"You *had* to get that telegram. Was your key open at 3:30?"

"Of course it was."

"3:30 their time?"

"Why shore, I was back from . . ." Josh stopped and his face fell. He fumbled with his GUIDE and found the map of time zones.

"That's 12:30 our time." He looked down at his hands, crestfallen. "I was at Delmonico's."

Doyle exhaled all his air, totally defeated. "All that work, all that planning, and your key wasn't open."

"Well, dadgummit, I got this system for my lunch . . ."

"Forget your system. Get onto that key right now, and send a telegram to Washington, D.C., Western Union Office, to George Hamilton Webster III."

Josh's heavy brows dropped. "George who?"

"You don't know who George Hamilton Webster III is?"

"Never heard of him."

Doyle gaped. "He's the chairman of the board of Western Union! He's the man who recommended you, and you're telling me you don't even know his name? You better get on the key and I'll dictate a telegram to clear this all up right now."

Josh sat down and started the tapping of his call numbers, then stopped.

Doyle stared. "What's wrong?"

"Washington's keys closed. It's after six o'clock out there."

"You mean . . ." Doyle looked horrified.

Josh's jaw thrust out defiantly. "Now jist a dang minute," he exclaimed. "You walk in here talkin' about secret telegrams and Pinkertons and King George and expect everything to go hunky-dory. Well you kin just fergit that. You want to send a telegram, say so. If you don't, I got better things to do, and if King George don't like it he kin lump it." Josh bobbed his head, for emphasis.

Doyle's mouth became a straight line. "You better get something straight," he purred. "My mission is at the request of the president of the United States. Our country is having trouble that could result in the biggest land war in history, and it all depends on two things. Secrecy, and total cooperation. The president contacted my father, and my father commissioned me to do this job. And George Hamilton Webster III said his man in Pocatello would do his share."

Josh reared back in his chair and choked out, "*Me?*" He swallowed hard and his Adam's apple disappeared. Doyle watched while his eyes grew larger and larger, and began to glaze. Suddenly Doyle noticed he was turning light blue and wasn't breathing. He reached over the counter and whacked Josh on the back. Josh's Adam's apple bobbed back into place and he sucked a great draught of air and his color returned.

"Yeah, you," Doyle said.

"The president of these here Yewnited States talked to your father? Who's yer father?"

"Allan Pinkerton."

"Never heard . . . wait . . . ain't it him started up the Pinkertons?"

"The same."

Josh swallowed hard again. "What's the plan?"

Doyle shook his head. "I can't tell you all of it. All you need to know is that it's possible we could get into a war with a neighboring nation over a border dispute, so I've got to have some telegraph equipment one hundred eighty miles northwest of here within six days to handle messages with the War Department in Washington, D.C. Time's running out."

"Canada!" Josh gasped. "We're goin' to war with Canada! I allus figgered we shoulda held out for the 50th parallel, not the 49th. What am I supposed to do?"

Again Doyle looked out the windows to be certain no one was near. "On pain of death, you are not to say a word of this to anyone. Here's my letter of authorization in case the coded telegram failed. You're supposed to read it and then I've got to burn it. If it fell into the wrong hands . . ." Doyle trailed off and his face became fierce and grim.

For a fleeting moment Josh saw destruction for the United States and death for himself. He reached for the sealed Western Union envelope. His hands shook while he opened it and his lips moved silently while he read, then re-read the terse, vital message addressed to him and inspected the flourished signature of George Hamilton Webster III.

"Where's the list this thing's talkin' about?'

Doyle solemnly handed the second envelope to Josh, who trembled while he opened and read it.

"The wagon? Mules? Dynamite? A runnin' iron? Supplies?"

"That's your part. We've got to keep the list, but you've got to read the authorization letter one more time and then repeat it to me."

Josh re-read the letter, and Doyle quizzed him. Satisfied, Doyle took the letter and burned it to ashes, which he ground into the pine floor. Doyle pointed at the list.

"That list is important. I've got to have what's there ready to go by tomorrow night. I leave at midnight. Wait about ten days and telegraph Webster at the Baltimore office of Western Union and ask him to confirm all this. I'll be gone by then, but he'll confirm it."

"Why am I waitin' ten days?" Josh scratched his stubble whiskers. "If King George is the big rooster at Western Union, what's he doin' in Washington? Why can't I telegraph him in the mornin' at Baltimore, first thing?"

"Webster's in Washington on secret invitation of the president, but he's leaving Washington tonight for Chicago to do his part of the mission. Ten days from now he returns to Baltimore, so you can't reach him until then. That's why! And if you try to contact anyone besides Webster, they won't even know what you're talking about and you'll likely ruin the whole thing."

"Oh," Josh said, and his face clouded. He fell silent, listening.

"Now what you've got to do," Doyle said, "is act like everything's normal. Get the food from Malloy's and the dynamite from the railroad and tell them all that stuff is for a big maintenance crew coming in and they're going to be gone with the wagon for a spell so you'll need thirty days credit. Keep all the receipts and Webster will tell you when to send them on to Baltimore and what secret code number to use on 'em. They'll get the money from the president himself and pay all the bills."

Doyle waited for five seconds while Josh digested that load, and then continued. "And in the meantime, you've got to teach me how to use all that equipment—those big batteries and the wires and switches in the maintenance wagon."

Josh cocked an eye. "You figgerin' me to teach you Morse code in one day?"

"No, the War Department's got a secret code that no one can decipher if it gets intercepted. That's what I use."

Josh looked at the clock, ballooned his cheeks and blew air. "I never heard of such a harebrained scheme, but I ain't got time to fret about it. It's after five now an' I got to git down to Molly's and the railroad station before they close if I'm to have these here supplies loaded by tomorrow evenin'."

Josh rose, scanned the two-column list once more, and Doyle followed him out the door and waited while he locked it.

"I'll come back in about an hour and you can show me the stuff in the maintenance wagon before it's dark," Doyle said.

Josh bobbed his head and scurried across the street to the railroad station. Doyle sauntered to the saloon and peered inside for a moment. Slade and part of his gang had their bellies to the bar and a foot on the brass rail, and no one noticed him. Doyle walked back out into the sunlight, then over to the hotel.

At 6:30 Doyle ate meat and potatoes at Delmonico's, then walked back to the Western Union office. Josh met him at the door.

"Come on," he said. "Let's get started."

Josh explained the huge batteries, their terminals, the hookups, and how to set the screws to connect the wires until dusk settled. Doyle lighted a lamp and hung it from the center post that supported the ridgepole in the shed, and turned to Josh.

"Okay. Let me give 'er a try."

It took Doyle five minutes to wind the wires around the positive and negative poles, work down the set screws, and hook them to the telegrapher's key that was bolted to the small workbench at the rear of the wagon. He stepped back to check his work.

"That should do it," he said quietly. "Here she goes."

He shoved the contact switch home into its receiver, and braced for the fireworks if he had wired it wrong. Nothing happened. He settled onto the small stool before the key, licked his lips, and looked at Josh. He gently lowered two fingers onto the wooden keypad and tapped.

It clicked.

A broad grin creased Doyle's face. "I think I got it."

"Yeah, you done good," Josh said.

"You know your stuff," Doyle said, and Josh grinned.

"How much electricity in those batteries?"

Josh pursed his mouth. "Depends on if they're carryin' a full charge, which these are. About a hundred and twenty volts."

"That enough to hurt?"

"Yeah. Knock you kickin', maybe kill you if it hits you right. Don't make no mistakes, and don't fergit to open that switch before you start messin' around."

"Yes sir. I'll run through this again early tomorrow. You did good. I sure do thank you."

Josh looked grand and shrugged. "Oh, weren't nothin'." He thought and then said, "Well, I guess it was somethin'."

"Yes it was. Why don't you head on home? I'll disconnect and put all this stuff away. I might try it once more tonight. No need to keep you here."

Josh looked doubtful. "You sure?"

"Yeah. Sure."

Josh walked out into the darkness while Doyle wound the thin, shiny copper wire into a large, loose coil. He dropped it to the dirt floor while he climbed into the wagon and crouched to loosen the thumb set screws.

They were inside the shed before he heard them.

"Well, now, what we got here?" Slade sneered, his face ugly in the yellow glow of the single lamp. Five of his gang were with him. The stench of sour whiskey filled the shed.

Without looking, Doyle slowly reset the thumb screws.

"You ain't got your coat on this time," Slade jeered, "so I don't reckon you got that Derringer."

Doyle neither spoke nor moved.

Slade's voice became loud, nasty. "I reckon you need a lesson. Maybe you won't be so disrespectful with a few scars on that pretty face to remind you not to mess with me."

Slade jerked his knife from its sheath and started forward, two of his mob with him. Doyle let his hand drop from the set screws to the open switch, and he waited.

On the second step, all three men put a foot down on the loose coil of wires, nearly invisible in the dirt, but still connected to the switch and the huge battery.

Doyle jammed the switch closed.

The buzz and the smoke and the three horrendous leaps all came in the same instant, followed by sounds akin to three wolves talking to the moon. The knife smacked into the ceiling and fell back to the dirt floor. Slade stopped rolling twelve feet from the tailgate, one of the others stopped ten feet out the door, and the third one careened off the front wheel of the wagon and lay in the dirt. Their feet were smoking, their eyes bugged, their bodies stiff as fence posts.

Doyle opened the switch and stepped out of the wagon. He faced the remaining three, who stood paralyzed, chins on their chests as they gaped, white-faced, in disbelief at the athletic abilities of their fallen comrades.

"You fellas want to try cutting up my face?" he asked casually.

Instantly all three shook their heads violently.

"Good. Tell you what. You three gather up your friends, and come with me. The 9:40 eastbound ought to be coming through about now."

He led them to the train station just as the

lonesome wail of the 9:40 reached out across the last mile before the station. The headlight came into view before the engine ground to a screeching halt, steam valves wide-open, blowing. The crew swung the arm from the water tower and started filling the boiler.

"What we're going to do," Doyle said, "is you three who can walk are going to load those three who can't onto the rods right over there under that cattle car. And then you're going to get on there with them, and you're going for a ride. A long one."

"But them cattle cars is loaded."

Doyle smiled. "Well, you just be nice and the cattle won't mind. Slade and those other two ought to start moving and talking along about sunup. I'm going to telegraph ahead to Utah, and if you get off before Colorado, there'll be a sheriff waiting."

None of the men moved. Doyle's smile disappeared and his next words were soft and low.

"Now git."

They sprang into action, and he watched as they carried the three stiff, still-smoking bodies to the railroad station and crammed them onto the rods and crawled in after them. The engineer blasted on the whistle, the train lurched forward, and was gone in the night. Doyle waited until it was out of sight and sound, and then turned his back on Slade and his gang.

The nasal voice stopped him in the middle of the street. "Hold on there."

Doyle waited for Pat to catch up and they walked on towards the maintenance shed.

Pat said, "I heard somethin' sounded like a cross

between a wolf pack and a tree full of panthers up here. What's goin' on?"

Doyle shrugged. "Slade and five of his friends decided to leave town. They was just hollerin' with joy there for a minute."

"How did they leave?"

"On the 9:40."

"Why?"

Doyle shook his head. "I don't know. It was kind of a shock."

"Say when they was comin' back?"

"Nope. Headed for Colorado."

Pat scratched his jowl. "Good riddance. It was goin' to happen sooner or later. Well, I got to get back. Got to 'supervise' tonight." His big grin cracked his face in the moonlight.

"You planning on winning?" Doyle asked.

"Yeah."

Doyle stopped and looked at him. "I'm letting you know I'm leaving late tomorrow. Don't tell anyone."

"Headed where?"

Doyle remained silent.

"Still on some secret government job, huh?"

Doyle said nothing.

"Well, stay out of trouble 'til you're gone."

Pat walked away and Doyle began dismantling the wires from the batteries. He finished and reached for the lamp. He was turning down the wick when a voice again froze him in his tracks.

"Mr. Doyle."

He pivoted and started to swing the lamp, and then caught himself. He sucked air and dropped his head forward, eyes closed in disgust.

"I told you, folks been killed sneaking up like that."

"I'm sorry," Molly said. "I heard something up here. I was worried. Are you all right?"

"I'm fine."

"I thought I heard Slade."

"You did. He's gone."

"Where?"

"Colorado."

"You ran him out?"

"Let's settle for the fact he's gone."

Molly looked up at him in the pale lamplight, her face framed in black hair. "It's a wonderful thing you've done, getting rid of him."

Doyle looked about the shed. "Everything's put away. I've got to lock up."

Molly stood directly in his path. "Josh placed a huge food order with me and he ordered six cases of dynamite from the railroad and some tools and other things around town. Said it was for a big maintenance crew coming in, but now I find you here. Somehow this all has to do with you."

Doyle closed the big doors, dropped the crossbar in place, set the huge lock through the rings, and snapped it shut.

"No, you're wrong. Now I've got things to do. Nice seeing you."

He turned the lamp wick down and started towards the hotel.

Molly hurried to walk beside him. "Have you talked to Wong?"

"I did."

"You'll take care of him?"

"I said I'd think about it."

"Please help him."

"I'll think about it."

"Do you know when you're leaving town?"

"No."

"Will you tell me when you know?"

"I'll just go. Then you can quit fretting."

Molly grasped his arm and pulled him to a stop. "No, I won't quit fretting. I can't. I need to know."

The silvery moonlight illuminated her upturned face like an angel, and for long moments Doyle stared into the bottomless pools of her eyes. He felt a rise within his breast that he did not understand, and he felt his breath come short. Suddenly he shook himself back to reality.

"Molly, I told you, don't do those woman things. It isn't fair. I'll be gone in the next day or two and that'll be the end of it."

He did not wait for a response. He pulled his arm free and quickly strode to the hotel. He sat on the bed in the dark for a long time, staring out through the lacy curtain into the silvery moonlight.

In deep twilight, Doyle dropped from the rear of the maintenance wagon to the ground and locked the tailgate in place.

"Looks like it's all there," he said to Josh. "Remember, keep all the bills, and in about ten days telegraph Webster in Baltimore. He'll get the money from the president in Washington."

Josh shook his head. "I don't know about all this. All that grub, and the dynamite and other stuff. And them two prime mules—they was a hunnerd and sixty dollars each. This better work."

"Yeah, it better," Doyle answered. "What we don't need in these parts is a shooting war." Doyle climbed into the wagon box and unwrapped the reins from the brake pole.

"You done good, Josh. I'll remember that in my report. It's possible I'll come back through here when I'm finished. You take care of yourself, hear?"

"I got a headache worryin' about all this," Josh retorted. "Six cases of dynamite. What if them mules stampedes and she blows?"

Doyle shrugged. "Then I won't be coming back through." He braced his feet and laid the reins to the rumps of the two tall, stocky mules, and hollered "Giddap!" and they leaned into the collars. The tug chains tightened and the wagon creaked and groaned into motion and the ground trembled.

Josh stood with his hands on his hips and watched the wagon turn east onto Main Street before he went back to close and lock the doors of the shed.

The tinny piano was yammering in the saloon, and the lights in the hotel lobby cast oblong patches of light into the street. Doyle held the mules to a steady walk and the ponderous wagon swayed slightly as it hit the potholes and ridges in the street. A flicker of movement in the shadows caught the corner of Doyle's eye and he turned to look at the darkened door of Malloy's store.

"Mr. Doyle!"

"Awww, fer cryin' out loud," Doyle muttered in disgust. He eased back on the reins and crooned "Whoaaaa!" The mules reared back and set their hooves and slowly stopped the wagon.

In the faint light of a nearly full moon just above the jagged mountain skyline, he saw four shadowy figures hurry from the boardwalk. Molly, Ping Fat, Fan, and Wong stopped by the front wagon wheel, beside the driver's box.

"Mr. Doyle," Molly said, "please take Wong."

"Now goldangit!" Doyle exploded. "I told Fan this morning I just can't do it, and that's final."

"You've got to. He won't stay in town without you. He has no one."

"And just what am I supposed to do with him? Tell me that!"

"Teach him. Get him to a new town where there aren't gangs that will abuse him."

"Slade's gone."

"There are others."

"I can't."

"Please." Molly reached up as though to touch Doyle's knee, and he jerked away, startled.

"Now don't do things like that," he said, "that isn't fair."

Molly spoke to Wong, and he scrambled up into the box, climbed over Doyle, and settled onto the wooden seat beside him. A giant grin split Wong's face.

"You're an angel, Mr. Doyle," Molly said.

He looked down at her upturned face. "I'm the dumbest human you ever saw," he exclaimed.

"An angel," she retorted.

He heard a softness in her voice, and it caught at him. He stopped and stared at her. She smiled and reached upward to him, and he impulsively stretched to grasp her hand for a brief moment.

"Thank you, Mr. Doyle."

"For being dumb?" he asked brusquely.

"For being Mr. Doyle," she smiled.

"Quit calling me Mr. Doyle," he retorted, irritated. "I'm Tim." Instantly his eyes widened in surprise and he wondered why he had invited her to the familiarity of using his first name.

She smiled up in the moonlight and repeated, "Tim," in a voice low and warm.

Doyle straightened and slapped the reins on the mules' rumps and gigged them back to a walk. He looked back once to see the three dim figures in the middle of the street, the tallest one waving until he was out of sight.

Half a mile east of town he turned north and the wheels of the wagon settled into the well-worn ruts of the wagon road leading to the Settlement. The moon was directly overhead before he hauled the mules in and made camp for the night.

The smell of coffee boiling and bacon crisping opened his eyes in the first light of dawn. Wong squatted by the fire, arms wrapped about his knees, waiting silently for Doyle to awaken. He saw the movement in Doyle's blankets and his huge smile gleamed in the growing light.

Ten minutes later Doyle was seated on a log finishing coffee, bacon, eggs, and biscuits while Wong watched Doyle's face for any sign of approval.

Doyle looked at the little man's round face, flat bridge to a button nose, long upper lip, little chin, and a frequent grin that was homely and fetching at the same time. Suddenly Doyle grinned, and then he laughed. Wong's eyes popped wide for a moment before he laughed too.

"I couldn't explain to anybody how I wound up here in the mountains with a Chinese I can't even talk to," Doyle said out loud. "But Wong, you can cook."

Doyle raised his plate. "Good. You savvy good?"

Wong grinned and nodded his head violently.

"Yeah, you don't savvy anything I say," Doyle said. "All you know is I haven't abused you." He sobered. "And maybe that's all any man really needs to know about another," he said quietly to himself.

He finished and started for the creek with his utensils but Wong leaped at him and grasped the tin plate and cup.

"Hey," Doyle exclaimed, "in my camp everybody takes care of themselves."

Wong tugged until Doyle yielded, and Wong trotted to the creek. Ten minutes later all the breakfast equipment was gleaming clean, packed in the wagon, and Wong was waiting to go.

In the late afternoon of the second day, as the sun reached for the western rim, Doyle stopped early in a high mountain meadow. Wong insisted on making all the meals, including supper, and soon had a pot of beef and potato stew warming in the black iron kettle over a small cook fire. Doyle dropped the tailgate of the wagon, swung up, and carefully reviewed the hookup Josh had taught him to connect the four big, 500 pound, black cast-iron storage batteries to the wires.

Twenty minutes later he had a thin copper wire strung from a battery to connect to a blasting cap and a stick of dynamite buried in an outcrop of rocks one hundred yards from the wagon.

"Wong!" he called, and the little Chinese trotted over, grinning as usual, and waited.

"You understand 'Boom'?"

Wong shrugged and tried the word under his breath. "Boom."

"Yeah. Boom. I'm going to teach you how to make a boom."

Wong said "Boom," and nodded, turning to go back to stir the stew, proud of his new vocabulary.

"Hey, come on back here," Doyle called. "We're going to *make* a boom, not *say* one."

Wong grinned and bobbed his head, completely baffled.

"Okay, here we go," Doyle said. He pointed to the switch on the big battery, and then grasped it between his thumb and forefinger, and waited for Wong to understand. Then he drove the switch home.

Flame leaped thirty feet as the blast and the concussion rolled past them. The mules jumped and brayed and Wong dived under the wagon with a finger in each ear, eyes closed, while a few shards of rock sprinkled the camp.

Doyle opened the switch and then hunkered down beside Wong to pull a finger from his ear. "Boom!"

Wong's eyes opened wide, and he bobbed his head half off. "Boom!" he repeated.

Doyle took Wong by the arm and walked to the tailgate, next to the big battery. Wong shrank back three steps, his large dark eyes filled with fear. Doyle grasped the switch again and turned to Wong.

"Switch. You understand switch? Say switch."

Wong silently mouthed the word, then tried it. "Switch."

"Good," Doyle exclaimed. "Watch what I do with the switch." Doyle did not notice Wong was standing with one foot on the wire when he pushed it shut.

The buzzing crackle came just before the whining sound, and Wong leaped four feet in the air and came down on his back. Doyle jerked the switch open and jumped to crouch beside the little man.

"Wong, Wong, you okay?" he cried.

Small curls of smoke drifted from Wong's feet, pigtail, and ears. His eyes were bugged, set, glazed.

His mouth was locked open and a hint of smoke drifted upward. His usually dusky skin was blue. He was not breathing. Doyle grabbed him, but he was rigid as a fence post from head to toe.

Doyle shook him desperately and then jammed his ear against the bony chest and held his breath, listening. One faint, timid heartbeat—seconds later another—and then it caught and the erratic beats began a regular rhythm. Wong coughed and began to breathe and slowly his color returned. Doyle slapped the small hands to help circulation, and finally Wong sighed and blinked and focused up at Doyle.

"Who you?" he asked softly.

Doyle released pent-up breath. "You okay?"

"Don't know. How I get here?"

"Lightning," Doyle said.

Wong looked at the cloudless early evening sky and a wistful disbelief shone in his eyes. He looked back at Doyle. "Was in China, talk with father, many ancestors."

Suddenly Doyle froze. "Hey! You're talking English. How'd you start speaking English?"

Wong looked at him in wonder. "I no talk English before?"

"Not a word."

"Huh!" Wong exclaimed with wonder. "How I learn?"

Doyle clacked his gaping mouth closed. "Maybe that lightning shook it loose."

"Possible. Lightning big surprise to Wong."

"I'll get some whiskey from the medicine chest. You sit here for a minute."

While Wong choked down a sip of whiskey,

Doyle connected two more sticks of dynamite and five railroad flares to the wire out in the rocks and came back to the wagon.

"Okay, here's the switch. Understand?"

"Wong no touch switch. Too much lightning."

"That was a mistake. Come on. You've got to learn to handle this switch."

Doyle coaxed him back, and Wong timidly locked his fingers onto the switch.

"When I say boom, push it closed."

Wong's fingers were trembling. "No push switch. When lightning come—Wong back in China, talk to ancestors. They say, no mess with switch. Switch bad."

Doyle looked fierce. "You push it or I cut off your pigtail!"

Wong shuddered, but held onto the switch.

"Okay. Here we go. Boom!" Doyle shouted.

Wong closed his eyes and jammed the switch closed. The blast dug a hole a foot deep between the rocks and blew the railroad flares 600 yards into the sky, burning like rockets. They arched outward and downward, leaving five perfect white smoke trails in the setting sun.

Wong leaped from the rear of the wagon and hid behind the mules. For five minutes Doyle pleaded with Wong before he would come back. Again Doyle rigged a stick of dynamite to the wire, and again he talked Wong back to the switch.

"Boom," Doyle cued.

Again Wong closed his eyes and shoved the switch, but this time he jerked his head up in time to see the flame spurt and the rocks jump. Suddenly he looked at Doyle in amazement, and a great grin spread over his face.

"Wong make boom!"

"You sure did! A good boom."

The little man jumped to the ground and stood straight, his shoulders thrown back. "Wong good boomer."

"Real good," Doyle assured him. "Now let's have supper." He spooned a heap of smoking stew onto his tin plate, poured coffee, and sat down on a log with a piece of hardtack. Wong settled beside him and picked at his stew with his fork for a second.

"Wong make more boom afta suppa?"

"We've boomed enough today."

"Afta suppa," Wong insisted.

"Tomorrow."

Wong's shoulders slumped.

When the supper dishes were finished, Wong sat dejectedly on the log. "Plenty too bad Wong no make anutha boom."

Ten minutes later Doyle stood out of sight, twenty feet from the wagon, while Wong crouched again beside the huge battery, thumb and finger in a death lock on the switch.

"Ready?" Doyle called.

"Wong plenty ready," the little man said, eyes bright.

From his hidden position, Doyle roared out in his strongest preacher's voice. "And the Lord God of Israel's voice came from heaven like the boom . . ."

Wong punched the switch home and the dynamite blew. He leaped from the wagon and danced a jig.

"Wong make anutha boom," he said loudly, beaming.

"Wong fine boomer," Doyle said.

"Wong make one more boom."

"Tomorrow."

In the rose colors of dawn, Wong pleaded and begged and Doyle reluctantly let him boom once after breakfast. Then they hitched up the jumpy mules and Doyle pointed them north once more, over the crooked, winding, rutted trail. They nooned at a spring and Doyle threatened Wong's pigtail if he asked to boom again, and they moved on with Wong's shoulders slumped sadly.

At dusk Doyle saw the Settlement from the high mountain pass, far away, below them. The Settlement. The tiny clearing that held the old Cataldo Mission, near where the setting sun made a twisting, golden ribbon of the mighty Snake River. Built by Spanish conquerors long forgotten, it had been wounded by cannon and rifle shot, and battered by each succeeding army that claimed this wilderness territory. He pulled the mules to a stop and gazed, awed and humbled by the rugged, unending sweep of the Rocky Mountains, jeweled with emerald pines, white-capped with eternal snows.

That evening they made camp, and Doyle unbolted the two boards from either side of the wagon that had the words WESTERN UNION burned in the wood. Doyle worked late with the running iron, heated red in the cooking fire. Wong watched in fascination as smoke rose from the letters Doyle burned into the blank sides of the two boards.

Wong stared at the neat, even words after Doyle bolted the boards back onto the wagon with his new signs facing outward.

"Many words," Wong said. "What words say?"

"That says 'Royal Maccabees Rocky Mountain Salvation Company'," Doyle answered.

"What that?"

"The Maccabees are out of the Bible." After supper, Doyle seated himself on a log beside the fire, poring over the great Bible from Malloy's. The fire burned low before Doyle stretched and carefully placed the Bible back under the wagon seat, and sought his blankets.

Dawn found Doyle seated in the wagon gazing through the crisp, clear, high mountain air at the Settlement. He turned to Wong beside him, waiting patiently.

"Well," he said, pointing. "That's where we're going. Things are likely going to get tense before we finish. You ready for this?"

"Wong ready," the little man said through his grin.

"You're going to need a new, Christian name." Doyle reflected for a moment. "Joshua. While we're down there, we'll call you Joshua."

"Wong Joshua?" the little man asked, his face clouded.

Doyle smiled. "No, just Joshua. You'll need that name to do what we're going to do."

"What we going to do down there?"

Doyle licked his lips. "Mine for gold."

He straightened his new, low-crowned black hat squarely on his head, adjusted his black string tie against the breast of his new white shirt, and straightened his new, black, knee-length frock coat. Then he put the leather to the mules and the wagon rumbled forward, down the high mountain trail, across a wide, grassy valley sprinkled with lodgepole pines, then down into the clearing by the remains of the thick walls of the old mission. Doyle pulled the mules to a stop twenty yards from the crumbling old building and waited, warily watching for anything to move.

A robust, handsome, auburn-haired woman stepped from the scarred door and shaded her eyes to look. She wiped her hands on her apron and walked out to meet them. A girl, a copy of the woman, followed, holding firmly to the hand of a toddling tow-headed boy.

"Howdy," the woman said. Her voice was big, warm, genuine. "Welcome to the Settlement. I'm Kate. These young'uns are mine, Sarah and Clyde. Step on down."

Doyle wound the reins around the brake pole, tucked the Bible under his arm, and stepped to the ground and walked purposefully to the woman.

"It is a pleasure to meet you, ma'am. I am Abraham Isaacson." He glanced down at the chidren who were smiling shyly behind Kate's skirts. "Beautiful children."

Kate thrust out her hand and shook his warmly. "Nice to meet you, Mr. Isaacson. Come on in and have a cool drink of sweet cider. Bring your companion. My husband Trace is due back directly. He's in the freight business, him and Pike."

Doyle spoke to Wong, who climbed to the

ground and followed them through the door into the spacious room with the rich smells of a general store. Kate set five cups on the counter and poured cider.

"Ma'am, this is Wong. His Christian name is Joshua." Doyle gestured to Wong, who bowed repeatedly.

Kate bowed back and shook his hand vigorously. "My pleasure, Mr. Wong. Or Joshua."

Wong shook her extended hand and bowed twice more.

"Wong speaks very little," Doyle said. "He was nearly the victim of a mob when I found him. I think it is part of my mission to educate him."

"Passin' through?" Kate asked, with her generous smile.

"I'm following the spirit. I believe I have a call to a ministry in these mountains but I don't know where, yet."

"Well," Kate said, "you're welcome as the sunshine. We don't get many of your kind in here. Hardly enough people for a congregation, 'cept for the Blackfeet."

"Indians?"

"Yep. Got a bunch of 'em not far from here. But I don't reckon the spirit is going to guide you to a collection of Indians."

Doyle paused with his glass half-raised and his face became solemn. "Remarkable!" He slowly settled the glass back on the counter. "You have awakened something inside me. It is possible I am supposed to serve the Blackfeet. I will have to pray about it and wait for my answer."

Kate shrugged. "You can sure stay around here

while you're waitin'. Be right honored if you'd give us a preachment or two from the Bible."

"Perhaps the spirit guided me here to receive your thoughts. I do thank you."

They finished their cider, and Doyle drove the wagon to the well, unhitched the mules, and set up camp. With the glow of the western sun setting the tops of the pine trees ablaze, two great freight wagons, drawn by six teams of mules each, rumbled into the clearing and Kate trotted from the old mission.

She threw her arms about the taller man who was driving the first wagon. He wore jeans with suspenders and a woolen shirt. He swept Kate off the ground in a bear hug and kissed her. He set her down and stooped to lift the two children, one on each arm. They threw small arms around his neck and covered his face with kisses.

Kate turned and hugged the second driver, who was short, barrel-chested, with legs like tree stumps. His bearded face cracked in a huge, gap-toothed grin. She locked arms with the taller man and walked the group over to Doyle and Wong, her face beaming with pride and joy.

"Mr. Isaacson, this here's my husband, Trace. And this other runty no account is Pike."

Pike's laugh echoed in the pines and they shook hands all around.

Trace looked at the sign on the sideboard of Doyle's wagon. "You're a minister?"

"Yes."

"You're staying for supper, aren't you?"

"I couldn't put that burden on you."

"Won't have it any other way. Kate, what do you say?"

Kate set venison, ham, roast, and potatoes plus peas and greens in steaming bowls and followed it with mountain blueberry pie, and cool pitchers of milk on the table. The talk flowed while everyone devoured the abundance.

Trace settled back in his chair. "The wagon says 'Royal Maccabees'. I don't think I ever heard of the Royal Maccabees religion."

Doyle replied, "It's Biblical. They were a very secret organization."

"Where are the Maccabees from?" asked Kate.

"Around Jerusalem," Doyle answered.

Kate stood. "After we get the table cleared, would you give us a little sermon from the Bible?"

They all helped clear the table and then each took their place again. Doyle bowed his head in a moment of deep reflection, then began turning the pages of his large Bible.

"I will take just a few moments of your time to reveal to you the workings of the Maccabees. This is taken from the book of Matthew, chapter 26. It tells of the betrayal of Jesus by the villain, Judas."

Doyle placed his finger on the page and continued while his finger followed the printed lines.

"After the betrayal, the soldiers seized our Lord, and verse 51 tells us that one of them which was with Jesus stretched out his hand and drew his sword, and struck a servant of the high priests and smote off his ear."

Doyle closed the Bible with deliberation.

"That single man who drew his sword to defy

the evil horde was a Maccabee. Since that moment, we have never failed in our devotion to the cause."

Kate's face clouded for a moment and she said, "I thought the man who pulled the sword was Peter. Doesn't it say that somewhere?"

Doyle looked at her solemnly. "Peter was a Maccabee."

"But," Kate said, "I thought Peter was a fisherman."

Doyle cleared his throat. "The Maccabees accepted all who would dedicate their lives and worldly possessions to the Lord Jesus. Their members came from all walks of life."

Trace glanced at Kate, then looked back at Doyle. "I don't remember ever hearing about the Maccabees in the New Testament."

"That's how secret they were," Doyle answered, and stood up abruptly.

"Joshua and I surely do thank you for your hospitality. If you'll just tell me how to find those Blackfeet, I'll be on my way before dawn."

Trace pointed. "Right on west about eight miles. Can't miss 'em. Their village sits right where two creeks meet. They're friendly so there's no need to fear."

Doyle left his blessing on the house and walked out into the velvety night with Wong beside him.

Trace and Kate watched them until the lantern began to glow inside the wagon, and Kate looked up at Trace. "Somethin's botherin' you."

"Yeah. Let's take a look at the Bible."

Twenty minutes later he called to Kate. "The Maccabees were Jewish fighters that lived during

Old Testament times. They were all gone before Jesus was born."

Trace slowly closed the big family Bible and leaned back in his chair. "Brother Isaacson out there doesn't know much about the Maccabees, and that Bible of his looks like it's hardly ever been used." He stood and stretched. "I wonder who he is and what he wants. Keep a sharp eye."

When the first rays of the sun crept over the eastern mountains and magically transformed the Settlement into a glowing gem for a few moments, Kate opened the door and stepped out into the crystal clear mountain air. For a moment she listened to the jays declare another glorious day, and the chatter of the squirrels and chipmunks.

She looked around the clearing and felt a sense of loss. The Royal Maccabees wagon was gone. All that remained were the tracks of the broad wheels and the mules, leading due west.

"Whoaaa!" Doyle called to the mules and hauled back on the reins. The mules sat back on their haunches, and the wagon swayed to a stop in the afternoon sun.

A great, open meadow spread before them, ringed with lodgepole pine, covered with rich grasses and high mountain summer flowers. A quiet stream flowed from the north, joined by a smaller one from the east, and more than fifty teepees clustered about the place where they converged.

For long minutes Doyle studied the Indians moving about the village. They were all sizes and descriptions—children playing, women weaving reeds into baskets, men slicing venison for the drying racks.

Doyle looked at Wong, seated next to him, and exhaled a deep breath. Wong's loose canvas shirt and baggy pants were washed and clean, and his old sandals hung on his bare feet.

"Joshua," Doyle said, "this is where we find out if we strike gold, or get scalped. Ready?"

Wong's eyebrows raised in guarded hope. "Make boom?"

"Later. I promise. Big boom."

Doyle gigged the mules, and the wagon

lumbered down the slight incline into the village. Children ran to meet him, clapping hands and chattering. Women followed, smiling, nodding apologies for their bumptious offspring. Men paused to watch the great wagon rumble into the village.

Doyle stopped next to a ring of rocks that circled the huge ceremonial firepit at village center. He wrapped the reins around the brake pole and stood in the wagon box, Bible clutched under his arm, face solemn, while he gravely cast a judgmental eye on everyone.

The giant Lump, who had loaded the whiskey barrels at the livery barn back in town, appeared from behind a teepee to the right, eyes wide with curiosity. The hawk-nosed one who had outwitted the moonshiners emerged from the communal council lodge with a corncob pipe clenched between his teeth, and followed by the little Indian with nervous eyes.

Doyle lowered himself majestically to the ground, Bible locked under his arm. His hat was level and low, and he raised his hand to the square in the universal peace sign.

"Peace be unto you, my brothers."

He waited.

The hawk-nosed Indian removed the pipe from his mouth and squinted an eye. "Welcome. Who you?"

"I am Abraham Isaacson. Do you speak English?"

"Some." He looked at the wagon, and his eyes stopped on the letters burned into the wood while he tried to read the words. "You want food?"

Doyle stood firm, feet planted apart. "No. What is your name?"

"Charlie."

"That is a Christian name. What is your Indian name?"

Charlie's face puckered in puzzlement. "Charlie."

"Are you a Christian?"

Charlie cast a glance at the little Indian next to him for a moment, then shrugged. "Don't think so."

"I must talk with your chief."

Charlie reflected. "No chief. Medicine man. Shaman." He nudged the nervous-eyed Indian next to him and jabbed the stem of his corncob pipe at a small, low lodge made of willows and leaves. The small Indian darted to the lodge and called through the low entryway, then stood back.

The ancient blanket covering the entryway moved, and a bent, old figure pushed through and straightened. The lined, weathered face could have been one hundred years old. His watery old eyes were sunk in a mass of wrinkles. A prominent nose divided his face, and nearly hid a lipless mouth. He wore a white shirt with food and drink stains on the front and buttoned at the throat. His dark woolen trousers bagged at the knees and nearly covered his lace-up oxford shoes. He walked slowly on legs bowed with age. He stopped before Doyle and waited.

Doyle bowed slightly. "I am honored."

"You are welcome here," the old man said, and his voice had the feel of the wind in the pines. "For what reason you come?"

"I bring a message from the Great Spirit. A message of power. Great power."

The old mouth puckered for a moment. "The Jesus message?"

"Yes. And more."

"Catholics, Jesuits, Mormons already bring the Jesus message. Message of love. Then they all fight. Strange. Your message Christian too?"

"I am a Maccabee."

"No hear Maccabee before. What is Maccabee?"

"Servants of Jesus. Come to help."

The old face puckered. "Help do what?"

"Serve your fellow man."

"We try serve white man. He come to make treaty. Treaty say, we keep land, they leave us alone. Then they take more land, make new treaty. Make treaty fifty-four. All say, we keep land, they leave us alone. Now they got land, no leave us alone. Hard to serve white man." He shook his head sadly.

Doyle nodded slowly. "I come with much power to serve your people. Help change treaty with white man."

The old man scratched his gnarled throat for a moment. "You got power to change white man? Make him obey his treaty? Get land back for Indian?"

For long moments Doyle solemnly gazed at the people. "Plenty power. Make strong man weak. Make thunder. Make great sign in sky. Change mountains. Change rivers. Plenty power. Get land back for Indian. Change treaty."

The old eyes looked up and down at Doyle. "Where you get power?"

"Power come from Great Spirit."

"Tell Great Spirit show power now." The old eyes stared and the mouth became a straight line.

Doyle nodded his head slowly for a few seconds. "I ask Great Spirit what He say about showing power now. You wait."

Doyle climbed over the tailgate into the wagon and reeled 50 feet of fine copper wire from a spool and quickly attached it to the battery. Then he knelt, bowed his head, and raised his voice in loud prayer.

"Oh Great Spirit, I am your humble servant, Isaacson of the Maccabees. I ask now that you give me power to serve my fellow men, the noble Blackfeet."

He waited in silence for fifteen seconds, then climbed back out of the wagon with the end of the copper wire in his hand.

"Great Spirit speak to my heart. He says He will let me show you small part of his power. He says He will send his power in this wire."

The old Shaman looked at Doyle for a moment, then reached to grasp the wire. He waited, then shrugged.

"No power. Great Spirit must be white man."

"Great Spirit say, strong man must hold wire. Strongest man in village."

Shaman motioned to Lump, who walked to his side.

"Strongest man," Shaman said. "Pick up wagon. You want to see him pick up wagon?"

"No," Doyle said quickly. "First, Great Spirit say I must make sacrifice. Must pour water on earth."

Shaman spoke to the women and in a moment half a dozen clay water jugs appeared. Doyle poured a large puddle of water onto the ground a few feet from the tailgate.

"Tell strong man to stand in water."

Shaman signed and the giant obediently planted both feet in the water and mud.

"What his name?" Doyle asked.

"Lump."

"Tell Lump hold small wire in both hands. Very tight so he feel power."

Shaman gestured and spoke, and Lump grasped the wire in his huge paws and smiled.

"Now I talk with Great Spirit. He send power."

Shaman shrugged. Doyle climbed back into the wagon and again raised his voice. "Oh, Great Spirit, show us power." He jammed the switch closed.

The buzz and the whine from Lump and the gasps from the other Indians came all at the same instant. Doyle counted to three and opened the switch, quickly peering over the tailgate.

Lump stood stock still, hands in front of him, still locked onto the wire. His eyes were glazed and tiny wisps of smoke eddied from his moccasins. His eyes were bugged and his jaw was set, and he was not breathing. Doyle leaped to the ground and waved his hand in front of Lump's face.

There was no response.

Doyle pried the big hands off the wire and slapped the great cheeks until the eyes blinked, and Lump gasped and drew breath. Doyle stepped back and waited.

Lump's eyes finally focused on the wire at his

feet and he backed away. "Much power. Plenty power." His voice was raspy.

Doyle turned to Shaman. "Great Spirit say, twenty brave, strong warrior take wire, feel power."

Shaman turned and spoke and those nearest shook their heads. Shaman shrugged. "No have warrior. Blackfeet believe Jesus message—no fight, show love—no warrior."

Doyle looked perplexed. "Then Great Spirit say, bring twenty strong worker."

Shaman spoke again and twenty men reluctantly stepped forward. Doyle locked their hands on the wire, shoulder to shoulder. He climbed back into the wagon and again raised his voice in great prayer. "Oh Great Spirit, show power to these thy children" and shoved the switch home.

The buzz and the howls came together, and right on top of them came an ear-splitting burst of laughter. Doyle looked out over the tailgate.

In the history of the Blackfoot nation, there never was a sun dance, or a war dance, or a harvest dance, or any dance, like the one given by twenty men who were feeling the power of the Great Spirit. Faces contorted with howls, feet hit the ground so fast no one could count, eyes popped, arms gyrated as they tried to release the crackling wire; the men invented body contortions and dance steps theretofore unknown on the North American continent.

The rest of the village had their hands over their mouths trying to stifle the tide of laughter.

Doyle opened the switch.

Moccasins smoking, eyes wide with fear, the twenty men cast the wire down and backed away, watching it intently until they were ten feet back. They turned and ran to the rear of the crowd.

Doyle faced Shaman. "Great Spirit send much power. Send power to change treaty. Help Indian. Get land back."

Shaman stared at the wire and suddenly picked it up. He worked it with his hand, then dropped it. "Now make thunder, send sign in sky, change mountain, river. Get land back."

"That power take much prayer. Must talk with Great Spirit alone, at night. Great Spirit send that power tomorrow. Maybe next day."

Shaman considered. "You stay, talk Great Spirit until He send power."

Doyle looked towards the heavens for several seconds, then back at Shaman. "Great Spirit say I stay."

"Camp there," Shaman pointed.

Doyle and Wong set up their tent beneath a half dozen towering pines, while children watched and chattered. He led the mules into the thick grass near the stream southwest of the village and hobbled them. In late afternoon sunshine he watched the women stir steaming pots, and as the sun reached for the western mountains, the village gathered for their evening meal.

"You come," Shaman said to Doyle.

Doyle and Wong sat cross-legged before his hogan and ate venison stew and mountain blueberries and drank clear, cold, sweet water. After supper the village gathered at the ceremonial firepit and young people built a large fire. Shaman came with a leather pouch and waited for silence before he faced the four points of the compass and cast a pinch of powder to each direction while he uttered the ancient incantation of thanks to the Great Spirit for the gifts of the earth.

In late twilight the men and women joined hands and circled the cracking flames to the steady rhythm of drums, and sang their chants to the wind and the rain and the sun. Shaman sat near his hogan, wrapped in a blanket, the firelight reflecting in his ancient eyes.

The children surrounded Doyle and tugged until he joined them in the circle, and they taught him the simple steps. In full darkness the dancing ceased and men brought forth wooden buckets with dippers, and everyone took their turn dipping a ladleful of liquid.

Doyle wrinkled his nose and sniffed until he identified the unmistakeable smell.

"Moonshine!" he muttered to himself, and looked at Shaman with raised eyebrows.

Shaman explained, "Sacrament wine, like Jesus in Bible."

"Raw whiskey," Doyle said.

Shaman shrugged. "No get wine, so use whiskey."

Doyle fell silent. Shaman watched his people at the buckets for a few minutes, then suddenly raised his arm. The people stopped, and the men carried the buckets away. The Blackfeet formed one more circle, danced one time, and again Shaman raised his arm. The villagers each went to their separate teepees amid laughter and jostling.

Doyle sat beside Shaman until the village was

quiet. The wrinkled, aged face was like stone in the flickering light of the dying fire.

"I talk with Great Spirit now," Doyle said. "Alone, in forest."

Shaman nodded once without changing his expression, then rose and disappeared into his hogan.

Doyle stood quietly beside his wagon for twenty full minutes while the camp dogs quieted, and then in the silence he climbed in where Wong was waiting.

They worked quickly and quietly. By midnight Doyle had strung copper wire a thousand yards west to a gentle rise of ground, and connected it to two sticks of dynamite and one railroad flare. Wong followed, covering the wire with dirt and pine needles. By three o'clock in the morning, with the three-quarter moon settling towards the eastern skyline, he had strung another wire five hundred yards south from the dynamite, and a third one five hundred yards north, while Wong followed and covered the wires.

At four o'clock Doyle was back in his tent beside the wagon. At five o'clock he could separate the heavens from the earth on the eastern horizon, and fifteen minutes later he could make out individual pine trees on the distant mountains.

He walked briskly to Shaman's hogan and called a greeting. Shaman poked his head out the blanket door.

Doyle said, "Great Spirit say He show power. Now."

Shaman disappeared for a moment, then

emerged with an old, battered cowbell, which he shook loudly while the village awakened and gathered rapidly.

"Great Spirit tell Isaacson He show power now," Shaman proclaimed, and turned to Doyle.

"Get people to firepit," Doyle said, and while they gathered, he took Wong back to the wagon.

Doyle looked at him intently. "Boom. When I say boom, you make boom."

A smile split Wong's face like a melon. "Wong make plenty boom," he said, and climbed in the wagon and settled down with his hand on the switch.

Doyle walked back to the firepit and faced Shaman and the villagers.

"Great Spirit say, silence. Great Spirit say, I talk to Him, ask for power."

Shaman spoke and women silenced babies and youngsters fell into wide-eyed silence.

Doyle waited until there was no sound in the village, then turned his face toward the west and raised both arms and tipped his face to the sky.

"Oh, Great Spirit," he intoned in a great voice. "Show these thy children, the Blackfeet, that thou hast power. Show thy power. Show us a sign in the sky."

Shaman moved his feet and his face puckered.

Doyle paused, and fixed him with a fierce stare. Shaman froze.

"Oh, Great Spirit, tell us what we must do to please thee. Let thy mighty voice boom . . ."

Wong shoved the switch home.

The dynamite blast blew flame fifty yards in the air and the railroad flare left a fiery, white tail six hundred yards into the pale blue of the clear sky. Tiny shards and fragments of rock sprinkled into the trees.

Everyone in the village gasped and stood frozen, wide-eyed. Doyle held his pose, arms wide, face towards the heavens for half a minute while the white trail of the burning flare arched downward and disappeared. Then he lowered his arms. "The Great Spirit has given a sign in the sky. He has shown his power," he said to Shaman.

"Now change mountain, change river," Shaman said. "Show power to make white man obey treaty."

"Tomorrow. Great Spirit say tomorrow."

Shaman cocked an eye. "I wait one more day," he said.

That evening, after the ceremonial dance, and the sacramental moonshine, Doyle waited until the village was again still.

"I must go into the forest again to talk with Great Spirit," he said to Shaman. "Alone."

Shaman nodded and disappeared into his hogan.

At midnight Doyle led Wong away from the wagon, west through the trees. Loaded in their backpacks were 120 sticks of dynamite, sixty railroad flares, and sixty blasting caps. By four o'clock they had reconnected the wires at the blast site. Doyle bundled two sticks of dynamite together with a railroad flare until he had sixty small bombs ready to wire to the two copper threads each running a thousand yards east and west. Wong covered all the wires. By five o'clock they were back in their tent.

"I knowed it. Yessir, I knowed it right off! That mangy polecat swindled us. The whole town." Josh held the telegram with trembling fingers while he pored over the words once more. "Tar and feathers is too good. Hangin's what we're gonna do. I got to git this to Pat." He stood and marched out the door, down the middle of the street, his eyes blazing, chin thrust forward.

Sven glanced out the window of his barber shop with his razor poised. He caught a glimpse of Josh and hesitated for a moment to stare. "Ol' Josh looks like war," he said, and made the downstroke on the right side of Ebenezer Horseley's lathered face with the razor. Eb pushed the razor aside and leaned up in the barber chair to look.

"Someone sure tied a knot in his tail," he said, and settled back down. "Josh ain't looked like that since he got the dysentery back in '84."

"Yeah. Wonder what he's got this time."

Across the street, Molly stepped off the boardwalk in front of the store and lowered packages into the buggy of Matilda Dingel.

"Thank you, Molly," Matilda said and stepped into the driver's seat. "And don't you breathe a word about Ellie and Hubert. I gave my special oath of secrecy that I wouldn't tell no one about them plannin' to elope. Promise?"

Molly smiled. "Of course. Be careful on the drive home."

Matilda reached for the reins before she noticed Josh, and she stopped. "Why, would you look at Josh! Looks like he's seen a ghost! I wonder what got into him."

Molly studied the firm step as Josh angled towards the sheriff's office. "I can't imagine," Molly said. "He surely looks determined."

"Hmmmm," Matilda muttered, and fidgeted for a minute. "I reckon I have a duty to wait to see if there's something I can do for him," she surmised, and settled back into the seat to watch.

"Pat!" shouted Josh from the street. "Pat, you best get on out here and take a look at this here telegram. This here's a national scandal!"

Molly stepped back onto the boardwalk and turned to watch. Matilda cocked an ear to listen. Sven quickly finished Eb Horseley's shave and the two walked out into the street. The day clerk at the hotel poked his head out the door. Reverend Gorten stepped out of the church and stood peering. Half a dozen men sauntered out the saloon door, beer mugs and whiskey jiggers still in their hands. Ping Fat and Fan walked out the tent flap of the laundry.

"What's all the shoutin'?" Sven called.

"We been swindled! That's what all the shoutin's about," Josh yelled back, and he thrust out his chin while the crowd gathered.

"Who's we?" Sven asked.

"Pat, Molly, the livery barn, the railroad,

Western Union—dang near the whole town—that's who!"

"Did I hear someone say swindled?" Reverend Gorten asked, his face long and pious.

Pat pushed his door open and hitched a broad suspender over his shoulder. He squinted one eye at Josh while he tried to focus the other one. He stepped off the boardwalk into the street, in his stocking feet. "You'd think a body could catch a nap," he complained. "What's all this shoutin' about?"

"We been swindled. That low-down varmint ain't no Pinkerton man, and he ain't here on gov'mnt assignment, and he ain't got no authority from Western Union, and nobody in Washington ever heard of him!"

Pat slowed. "Who?"

"Did someone say swindled?" inquired Reverend Gorten again.

"Jeremiah Pinkerton, or Doyle, or whoever he is," Josh exclaimed.

"Who says?" Pat rubbed at his eyes, still blinking in the sunlight.

"This here telegram. That's who."

Pat smoothed the telegram and read it, then read it again. He scratched his jowls and puckered his mouth for a moment. "Looks that way," he said.

"Let me see that," Molly demanded and snatched the telegram away from Pat. For long moments she pored over it, then handed it back to Pat without a word. Her face clouded.

"Why," Matilda gasped, "the nerve of that brazen fake! Coming in here the way he done, deceiving everyone, stealing that way. And now he's near broke poor Molly's heart!"

Molly's lip trembled and Matilda spoke to her. "But I promise I won't breathe a word to anyone, Molly. I swear on my special oath of secrecy."

"Well," Josh continued loudly, and fixed Pat with a stern stare. "What you figgerin' to do about it?"

Pat worked at his shirttail. "Nothin'."

Josh jerked back. "What? You gonna let that flea-bitten coyote get away with it? He musta stolt near two thousand dollars worth of stuff from half the folks in town. That wagon, an' them mules, and all the grub from Molly's, and the Union Pacific dynamite and all."

"I can't go after him." Pat scratched his ample paunch.

"Why in tarnation not?"

"He's outta my jurisdiction by now."

"How do you know if you ain't follered him yet?"

"Well, it's been nigh on a week since he left, and one thing's sure. He ain't likely to hang around here if that telegram's right."

"He headed north. He's likely at the Settlement right now." Josh pointed emphatically.

"That's sixty miles. Outside my county."

"The Settlement ain't in no county. It's just there. You got as much jurisdiction as you need."

"I can't do nothin' official outside the Bannock County line, and that line's forty miles north, not sixty."

Josh's face reddened and his Adam's apple disappeared. His eyes glazed and his breathing stopped.

Reverend Gorten whacked him on the back and Josh wheezed as his machinery started again.

"Pat," Josh exclaimed, "you got to go git him and bring all that stuff back. If I don't git that wagon and them mules and them big batt'ries back before the next inspectors git here, they hold it outta my pay. I'll be workin' for Western Union until I'm a hunnerd and fourteen!"

Pat sucked his teeth. "My job don't include counsellin' folks on how to do business. It's yer own fault you turned that stuff over to him, and now he's left the county, and there ain't nothin' I can do about it without you gettin' a court order first."

Molly faced Pat, her hands on hips, eyes flashing. "You're afraid you'll miss your share of the poker game in the back room of your office! That's why you won't go."

Pat flinched and he glanced around for a moment. He leaned forward and said quietly, "Now Molly, there ain't no need to . . ."

Molly cut him off and plowed ahead. "You're going to get together a posse and go after him and you're going to bring him back here. Him and all the things he took from us."

Pat looked pained. "Now Molly, you know I can't do that. My job's to keep the peace *here,* and I can't do that if I'm gallavantin' around the countryside out of my jurisdiction."

"Your job's to protect us. Deputize Sven to watch the town while you're gone. Josh said Doyle headed north towards the Settlement, and if that's true, he's gone to swindle the Blackfeet out of all their gold."

"Tarnation!" Josh exclaimed. "That's what he's done! He was after them big gold nuggets all the time! There ain't no war with Canada!"

Pat worked his stockinged foot in the dirt. "Tell you what. I'll send a couple telegrams an' . . ."

"You'll get a wagon," Molly scolded and shook her finger, "and you'll get a posse and you'll start north in the morning."

Pat grimaced. "Molly, there ain't no sense stampedin' . . ."

"Do it, or Matilda will tell the county about the poker game in your back room. You won't get a single vote in the next election."

"Did someone say poker?" asked Reverend Gorten.

Pat looked up pleadingly at Matilda.

Her mouth became a narrow slit and she looked fiercely down her nose at him.

Pat looked at Sven. "Can you keep the peace for a few days?"

Sven pursed his mouth for a minute. "What's the pay?"

"Dollar fifty a day."

"I get your cut of the back room game?"

Pat nodded his head sadly. "Yeah."

"I got to have a deputy."

"What for?"

"To give orders to. Can't do no sheriffin' if I don't give no orders."

"Okay."

Sven looked at Eb. "You stand bein' deputized for a few days?"

"I get wages and my share of the poker game too?"

"Yeah."

"Then I'll stick around."

"Uh . . . did I hear poker?" inquired the reverend.

Pat grumbled, "I got to get a posse and some grub and stuff. I'll leave at first light." He turned to Molly. "And Matilda don't say nothin' to no one about nothin'."

Molly looked up at Matilda who nodded.

"Agreed." Molly dropped her hands. "Who are you going to get for your posse?"

Pat shrugged. "I don't know. Only had a posse once before, back in '77 when someone stolt Sommersby's prize sow. Found the sow rootin' in the mud down by the crick, but never did find out who stolt her."

"I'll go," Molly said firmly.

Pat recoiled. "You? A woman?"

Molly bristled. "I can handle a Winchester better than most men, and I can drive a team as well as you."

"Well, I . . ."

"I'm going. Who else?"

Pat looked at Josh.

Josh shook his head. "I gotta stay here on that telegraph key. Why, the president might send a telegram sayin' he's sendin' out the U.S. Cavalry to get this here skunk."

"You send a telegram to the Corinne operator and tell him to take all your messages. You're goin'."

He turned to the hotel clerk, the saloon bartender, and half a dozen other men. "You're all deputized. Be here at five in the mornin'. Bring your own shootin' irons and blankets. Ammunition and grub's free. I'll have a wagon waitin'."

Ping Fat looked excited. "Me go!"

Pat shook his head. "Naw, the town can't run without the laundry."

"Fan do laundry," Ping Fat exclaimed, and Fan nodded her head.

Pat shrugged. "Be here at five in the mornin'." He turned to Molly. "Satisfied?"

She smiled sweetly.

The black velvet dome of night faded to deep purple, and the skyline of the wildly beautiful eastern mountains slowly emerged. Within seconds the light skiff of clouds was fired with red and rose and the first arc of the sun pushed upwards and the golden light came flooding down.

Dressed in his black frock coat and black hat, Doyle strode to the lodge of Shaman and shook the ragged, ancient blanket that covered the entrance. Shaman appeared.

"I pray all night. Great Spirit say to me, gather Blackfeet at council firepit, and I show them my power. Mighty power! Greater than power of sun!" Doyle looked fierce.

Shaman swallowed and nodded to Lump and Mole. Two minutes later the entire village was assembled at the firepit; women held sleepy children in their arms, while others stretched awake.

Doyle pointed west. "Great Spirit show power there," he said loudly. "I pray, and you watch."

He climbed the tailgate into the wagon and dropped out of sight. He sat Wong in front of the switch. "Boom. You savvy?"

Wong nodded his head rapidly. "Savvy plenty good."

Doyle climbed back over the tailgate to the ground. He slowly surveyed the entire tribe and spoke loudly. “Great Spirit say, you be silent while Isaacson pray.”

The entire village became so silent Doyle could hear blue jays chattering in the trees, and a woodpecker hammered on a dead pine somewhere south. He raised his hands to the heavens, arms extended, and turned his face upwards. “Great Spirit, You have heard my voice through the night. You answered my prayer. You say You will show Your power to Blackfeet. Show Your power.”

He waited. Nothing happened. Shaman looked at him with one eyebrow cocked. Doyle continued. “Your servant Isaacson is asking again, O Great One. Show your power.”

He stopped again. The blue jays argued in the trees. Chipmunks chattered and scampered unchecked into the teepees and lodges to steal bits of food. Shaman shifted his feet and pursed his mouth.

Again Doyle raised his hands. “O Great Spirit, your humble servant Isaacson heard Your voice in the night. It said, show power at dawn. It is dawn.”

Shaman said, “Your Great Spirit no . .”

“Silence,” Doyle shouted without turning his face from the heavens. “Great Spirit speak to Isaacson now.”

Every eye turned to the heavens and deep silence gripped the entire village while they listened. Doyle stood for a minute as though in a trance. The Blackfeet began to move, murmuring.

Suddenly Doyle dropped to his knees, then

toppled onto his side and rolled onto his back, arms flung wide. His eyes closed and he lay inert.

Shaman looked at him for a few seconds, then nudged him with the toe of his moccasin. "Great Spirit make mistake?" he queried. "Send wrong power?"

Doyle moved his hands slightly, then his eyes fluttered open, and he spoke with a strained voice. "Great Spirit say, He show power stronger than sun only if he receive offering. Great offering."

Shaman scratched his grizzled throat. "He want ceremonial wine?"

"No," Doyle said in disgust, "not moonshine. Great Spirit say Blackfeet have treasure. Must give up treasure to get power from Great Spirit."

Shaman shrugged. "We give five wife, twenty horse."

"No," Doyle said. "Great wealth."

"Ten wife, fifty horse? Never give ten wife, fifty horse for anything."

"Great Spirit angry with Shaman. Say, already have enough wife, enough horse. Great Spirit say, Blackfeet have hidden wealth from mountain, no tell anyone."

Shaman scratched his chin and looked pained. "Tell Great Spirit, if he know Blackfoot have hidden gold, he must also know where gold hidden. No need Blackfoot to tell. Go get for self if He so powerful."

Doyle stood and his eyes flashed like lightning. "Blackfoot have hidden gold?"

Shaman shrugged. "Ask your Great Spirit. He think He know all."

Doyle's face became terrible. "Now Great Spirit angry. Strike earth with power. Great Spirit voice will boom . . ."

Wong jammed the switch home.

A thousand yards away, the entire western quadrant of the compass erupted in a gigantic roar as four cases of dynamite blew. Sixty railroad flares glowed orange and streaked six hundred yards into the clear morning sky, leaving white tails like ribbons behind. Rocks and dirt jumped three hundred yards upward and black smoke billowed, rising a thousand feet into the sky. Shattered rock shards arced three-quarters of a mile in every direction and began raining down on the village. The blast deafened everyone for several moments. The horses jumped and stampeded to the far end of the meadow as the air wave whooshed past the petrified villagers. They turned their backs and threw their arms over their heads and hunched over, trembling and terrified.

Shaman moved his arms from over his head and looked at the billowing black cloud rising in the sky, and the white flare trails, and listened to the rock fragments peppering down on the village. He swallowed hard.

Doyle spoke loudly. "Shaman want Great Spirit strike whole village with power?"

Open murmuring broke out.

"No strike village," Shaman said.

"Blackfeet have gold?"

"Much gold."

"Must give to Great Spirit. Then He not strike village. Use great power to get land back for Blackfeet."

Shaman looked at Doyle long and hard. "How give gold to Great Spirit?"

"Give to his servant, Isaacson. Great Spirit tell Isaacson what to do with gold, then make white man give Blackfoot back the land."

Shaman studied the dissipating black cloud and the fading white streaks, and then he looked into the faces of his villagers. He spoke abruptly to Lump and Charlie, and they looked at him dubiously, then gave orders to the others. Shaman looked at Doyle, then pointed at the ashes in the center of the ceremonial firepit. "Gold there."

Doyle's eyes popped.

Shovels appeared from teepees and the men began digging. By nine o'clock they had opened a hole eight feet across and four feet deep, and Charlie dropped in to uncover and remove the first eight pound nugget. By ten o'clock they had a pile of nuggets two feet high and three feet across. By noon, the hole was ten feet deep, and Lump handed up the last nugget. The pile was four feet high and five feet across.

Doyle stood as though in a trance. "At least two tons," he mumbled to himself. "Two tons of pure gold."

The entire village surrounded Doyle and the pile of gold. Lump climbed from the pit and Charlie came to stand with him. Children clung to their mother's skirts and men stood with stolid faces, eyes boring into Doyle.

Doyle looked stern. "Great Spirit say all gold. Is this all?"

Shaman said with finality, "Have no more now."

"Where get gold?" Doyle demanded.

"Belong to Great Spirit, up in mountain."

"How much more?"

Shaman paused a long time. "Much."

"Where?" Doyle asked again, and held his breath.

Shaman did not flinch. His answer was instant. "Gold belong Great Spirit. Isaacson ask Him. Great Spirit tell you if He want you to know."

Doyle was unable to find a way around the simple logic. "Load Blackfoot treasure in wagon," he said, and looked severe. "Isaacson take treasure into mountain, ask Great Spirit what to do."

"Gold not Blackfoot treasure," Shaman said slowly. "Gold white man treasure. Mother Earth Blackfoot treasure. You take white man treasure and get Blackfoot land back."

Doyle stopped short as understanding came creeping into his heart. The white man's world of gold, greed, and lust had no place with this simple people. They asked only to be left with their families, their Great Spirit, and their Mother Earth. Nothing more.

Shaman continued. "We load gold in wagon. You go talk Great Spirit, do what He say, use power to get land back."

An hour later the great wagon box was settled nearly to its axles with over four thousand pounds of pure gold loaded and covered with tarps. Doyle climbed into the driver's seat and collected the reins while Wong sat quietly beside him.

He spoke with great dignity to Shaman. "Isaacson go, do what Great Spirit say. Get land back."

Shaman stood wrapped in his blanket with the entire village behind him, and they watched Doyle whack the reins on the rumps of the mules. The mule's hooves dug small craters as they scratched to slowly start the laden wagon. They had travelled two hundred yards when Doyle turned to look back. The entire village was waving to him—men, women, children—he hesitated, then waved back.

A moment later he breathed deep and exhaled and suddenly broke into a huge grin. "Wong, we did it." He whacked the surprised little man between the shoulder blades. "We did it! More than half a million in gold back there, all ours."

Wong's eyes narrowed. "Ours?"

"Tomorrow morning we cut southwest and head for San Francisco just as fast as this wagon can roll. You'll have enough money to buy a restaurant in Chinatown."

"Restaurant?" Wong asked. "No want restaurant."

"Okay, a laundry. You savvy laundry?"

Wong shrugged indifferently. "Savvy."

The tracks were deep, and the mules were taxed as they moved through high, rippling grass, across the small valley into the emerald green of the timbered hills, traveling due west. At dusk Doyle stopped near a small spring and they made a simple camp. After supper he lighted a lantern and pulled back the tarp. He dipped water from the spring and washed half a dozen nuggets, burnished them until they gleamed and he stared at the pile deep into the night.

Dawn found him asleep, sagged against the side of the wagon, the tarp clutched in his hand.

Wong shook his shoulder. "We go?"

Doyle jerked awake and for a moment stared at the nuggets as though he had dreamed them. He rose, stretched cramped muscles, and went to the stream to wash. He helped Wong with fried potatoes and eggs for breakfast.

With the dishes cleaned and packed, Doyle walked to the wagon and stood with both hands hooked over the tailgate, head bowed in deep thought. He dropped the tailgate, climbed in, and once again loosened the tarp to stare at the treasure.

He went to the front of the wagon and sat on the wagon tongue, hands on his thighs. He gazed for a long time eastward, at the wagon tracks that merged in the distance. In his mind he still saw the Blackfeet—the mothers and children, men, the old Shaman—standing clustered about the ceremonial firepit, their dark eyes pleading as they waved to him while the wagon rumbled away with their gold.

Wong sat down beside him. "No go Chinatown?"

For a long time Doyle did not move or speak. Then he raised his eyes to Wong. "I don't know. What do you say?"

Wong pursed his mouth for a moment. "Go get land back for Indian."

Doyle locked eyes with the little Chinese. In the dark eyes of the small man he saw the deep pain shared by all who ever suffered at the hands of unrighteous men who controlled wealth and power.

"I think I'm crazy," he said softly. "I think you're right, but I think I'm crazy."

Doyle hooked up the mules while Wong scrambled back onto the driver's seat. Doyle shouted and gigged the mules to a walk, and turned them hard left, traveling southeast.

Wong sat silently for the first mile, then turned his face to Doyle. "Go back?"

"We're going to get some land back for the Indians."

A huge smile spread over the round face.

* * *

Eight miles due east, at the Settlement, Kate paused in her kitchen to listen to a distant sound, and felt vibrations in her feet. "Trace, I think we got company on the way," she said.

Trace walked out into the clearing and listened for a moment, then looked east. Two wagons were rumbling in and Trace peered intently. He saw a dark-haired girl stand in the driver's box and wave, and then he saw the sheriff's badge on the vest of the driver. He hurried back to the house.

"Kate, the sheriff's driving the lead wagon and Molly's with him. I wonder what this is all about."

"Thunderation!" Sven's head jerked forward and his mouth dropped open until his chin was on his chest. He stood gaping out the window of his tonsorial parlor with his razor poised over the lathered face of Reverend Gorten.

"That's him!" he exclaimed, and gestured wildly with his left hand. The reverend's eyes never left the razor in Sven's right hand, trembling twelve inches above the reverend's throat.

"Half the town out chasin' around in the hills lookin' for him, and here he comes big as life, right smack dab up Main Street drivin' that wagon he stolt! The gall of that man."

"Sven," the reverend murmured, watching the razor repeatedly rise and fall several inches as Sven talked.

Sven suddenly jerked straight and his eyes popped. "I'm the law! I got to arrest that man! That means I got to go give Eb orders! Can't arrest nobody without I give Eb orders first!"

He folded the razor shut and tossed it on the back counter and the reverend's eyes closed in blessed relief. Sven headed for Pat's office where Eb had been napping with his feet on the desk. The reverend followed Sven out and stopped on the boardwalk to watch, squinting against the bright, mid-morning sun.

Eb barged out the sheriff's door before Sven got there and jabbed a finger towards the wagon. "That's him!" he exclaimed to Sven.

"Dadgum right that's him," Sven said. "A borned killer and thief! You got to arrest him!"

Eb stepped back, his hands up. "Now hold on there, you're the one in charge while Pat's gone. I'm just the assistant."

"You got to obey orders, and I'm orderin' you to arrest that man!"

"No, *you* arrest him. I'll stand right there behind you and assist."

"Eb, don't be stubborn! You already got paid for a week and didn't do nothin', and now I'm orderin' you in my official deputy capacity to arrest that man!"

"An' I'm tellin' you in my official capacity as your assistant that I'm hired to assist—and I'm willin' to do it—but you're the one has to make the arrest. Besides, you never paid me my half of the poker percentage from two nights ago."

"I told you, there wasn't no game! Homer got the bellyache and Zeb's wife got mean, and there wasn't no game! Now stop bein' ornery and make the arrest."

Doyle hauled the wagon to a stop in the middle of the street and looked at Sven and Eb. He dropped to the ground and started walking towards them. Doors opened and people filled the boardwalks on both sides of the street to watch. The saloon emptied.

Eb went white, then gray, and started backing up. Sven swallowed hard and stood rooted to the spot.

Doyle said, "What's wrong with you guys? Where's Pat and Josh?"

Eb was speechless, but Sven stammered, "P-P-P-Pat's gone and J-J-Josh went with h-h-h-him."

Doyle studied them both for a moment. "Sven, you're sure talking funny. You all right? Look a little peaked."

"We're f-f-f-fine."

"Where'd they go?" Doyle continued.

"H-h-h-h-huntin'," Sven blurted.

"Hunting?" Doyle looked puzzled. "Hunting what?"

"D-d-d-deer. R-r-r-rabbits."

"There's something wrong here," Doyle mused, and looked up and down the street. "Where's Molly?"

"H-h-h-h-huntin' with P-P-Pat."

"Molly went hunting? Not likely. What's gone wrong with this town?"

"Yer under arrest!" Eb blurted and took two steps backward, terrorized by his own outburst.

Doyle looked at him and broke into laughter. "Eb, you trying to arrest me?"

"No sir, oh, no sir, I ain't, I'm just tryin' to assist Sven. Pat put him in charge when he left with Josh and Molly and half the town to go lookin' fer you. Sven's makin' the arrest, not me, no sir, not me. Ain't that right Sven?"

Sven turned on Eb. "I told you to make the arrest and I'm in charge, so *you're* the one makin' the arrest. Go on. Git him."

"Now goldang it Sven, that wasn't how we agreed. I was just hired for a day or two to assist . . ."

Sounds of incoming wagons and horses came rumbling and every eye in town turned to look up Main Street. Sven's eyes grew big, then he heaved a great sigh of relief.

The two leading wagons had the canvas tops pulled off and eight or ten men sat in the box of each, rifles poking in the air. Pat drove the lead wagon, Molly seated beside him. Josh drove the second one, Trace drove the third one, with Kate by his side. The last wagon was driven by Charlie. Lump and Shaman and half a dozen other Indians sat in the box.

Doyle stood with his hands on his hips, feet spread slightly. "What are they all doing?" he wondered aloud.

"Pat and Josh and them folks with the rifles went lookin' fer you," Eb said before he thought. "They figger to lynch you."

"Well," Doyle said without moving, "they found me."

"They shore did," Sven said, "just in time to make the arrest."

In the lead wagon, Pat's head suddenly thrust forward. He stood and pointed at Doyle and said something to Molly. She gasped and clapped both hands over her mouth. Pat shouted at the horses and whacked them with the reins and urged them to a run, dust rising like a rooster tail behind the wagon. He hauled the horses to a stiff-legged halt ten feet from Doyle and the dust came rolling over all of them. Pat hurried down from the wagon as fast as his portliness would allow. He quickly strode to Doyle and stopped with his nose two feet from Doyle's. He puffed up as big as he could.

"Yer under arrest!" he exclaimed. "Fraud, grand theft, mule stealin', impersonatin' someone you ain't, embezzlement of railroad property, and interferin' with the Western Union."

Doyle looked bored. The other wagons emptied. Everybody bunched around Pat and Doyle, waiting expectantly on tiptoe to watch the arrest of the desperate outlaw and feared swindler, Doyle.

Pat looked ferocious. "What do you say to them charges?" He fished his handcuffs from his hip pocket.

"I did 'em all," Doyle said.

Pat froze. "You what?"

Doyle shrugged. "I did it."

Pat deflated and his shoulders sagged. "Doyle, you ain't supposed to say that. You're supposed to deny it so's we can have a trial and all like that."

"Sorry, Pat. I did it. All of it. And more."

Molly's eyes dropped and her chin trembled.

"You mean what Shaman told us?" Pat still fingered the handcuffs.

"Yep."

"It's true? You got some of them gold nuggets?"

The hush was instant and complete. Utter silence gripped everyone on Main Street as they strained to listen.

"Right there in the wagon," Doyle said.

Everyone caught their breath and waited for the next question.

"How . . ." Pat's voice cracked and he tried one

more time, but the words came out in a hoarse whisper. "How, how, how many?"

"Oh," Doyle mused, and scratched behind his ear. "I'd guess just over two tons."

For five seconds no one moved or spoke. Doyle walked to the wagon, dropped the tailgate, and peeled back the tarp. The sunlight caught the gold nuggets and everyone exhaled their breath and stood gaping as though hypnotized by the sparkling treasure. Pat's mouth began to water and he swallowed and started toward the gold.

Doyle jerked the tarp back in place and quickly slammed the tailgate. "Leave it right where it is, Pat," he warned. "I got a little work to do and it includes this gold."

Pat's voice came back. "That there gold is contraband and it's in my jurisdiction, so I gotta take custody."

"That gold is not contraband," Doyle said. "That is Blackfoot gold entrusted to me to do a job for the Blackfoot nation. And I'm going to do it."

Doyle looked at Shaman, and slowly the old Indian walked forward, and Doyle spoke. "Did you turn that gold over to me to get back the land the whites stole from you in those last fifty-three treaties?"

Shaman solemnly nodded his head. "You promised Great Spirit have power to get land if we give gold."

Doyle cocked one eye at Pat. "And that's just what I'm going to do."

"Naw," Pat exclaimed, "you're just workin' on one of your swindles again. I ain't figgered out what it is, but I'm takin' custody of that gold 'til I do."

Doyle turned to Shaman, who nodded at Lump, who walked to the tailgate of the wagon and turned to face the crowd.

"Go ahead, Pat," Doyle said. "Take it if you can."

"Now goldang it, that ain't fair. And it ain't legal, neither."

"It's Blackfoot gold with a Blackfoot protecting it. Tell me what's not fair or legal about that."

"Well, you got them Injuns hoodwinked. They don't know what they're doin'. That's what ain't fair."

"You got it all backwards, Pat," Doyle said. "The white men out here been hoodwinking those Indians for the past forty years, and for the first time the Blackfeet do know what they're doing. You go ahead and try to arrest someone, or take that gold, and when Lump finishes, half this town won't be standing. Make your move or back off."

Pat's face fell. "There's somethin' wrong here. I'm supposed to be arrestin' you and gettin' all that gold."

"Pat," Doyle said loudly, "how would you like to be part of a deal to give these people back what the whites stole from them? I mean a deal with the president of the United States? I can't think of anything more likely to get you re-elected."

Pat's eyes popped. "You're crazy."

Molly stepped forward, face filled with sudden hope. "Tim Doyle, do you mean you really are going to get the land back for these people, like you promised?"

"I sure mean to try."

"This isn't just a big scheme, like everything else you did around here?"

Doyle looked her in the eye. "I been conning and swindling people half my life. I swindled Josh and the railroad, and you, and half a dozen others in this town. I swindled the Indians, and I was headed for San Francisco with that gold when something happened. I don't know what it was, but I couldn't go through with it. I'm going to get their land back if I can like I promised."

"Tim Doyle, don't you lie to me." Her hands were on her hips and her eyes flashed.

"Now Molly, you be gentle. Here's what we're going to do. I figure seven of those nuggets will be just about fifty pounds of pure gold. I'm delivering them to Molly to pay everybody what I owe them for all the stuff I took, and there should be enough left over to divide among them for a little extra, just to be fair.

"When I finish at the telegraph office, I'm giving the wagon back to Josh. He can return the stuff in it to whoever owns it, and keep the wagon." He paused for a moment. "But right now, Josh and me are going down to the telegraph office. We're going to make a deal with the president of the United States. Pat and Shaman, you better come. Might come in handy."

Doyle remounted the wagon and was reaching for the reins when Molly climbed up beside him. Doyle looked at her surprised, and Molly looked back at him defiantly. Doyle turned the wagon and gigged the mules back up the street while the others followed on foot.

He stopped at the telegraph office, threw open the door, and walked in. Shaman and Pat followed and lined up at the counter: Molly next to Pat, Wong next to Molly, and suddenly Fan appeared next to Wong.

Josh took his place at the telegraph key while Doyle began writing. People crowded into every corner. Someone opened the windows so others could hear, and the crowd gathered in the street.

Doyle looked at Shaman. "Better send Lump out to watch the gold."

Shaman spoke and Lump walked out.

Doyle turned back. "Josh, sign on and get the president on his key in Washington. His name's Grover Cleveland. Tell him to get whoever runs Indian Affairs back there and bring all fifty-four treaties with the Blackfeet Indians, pronto. If anyone gets smart with you, tell 'em we've got the makings of an Indian war out here, and we got one Indian who can lick the whole U.S. Army." He looked outside at Lump and smiled, then continued writing. He finished and thrust the message to Josh. "Got the president yet?"

"His operator's waiting."

"Send him that."

Josh read it aloud. "The Blackfoot nation has fifty-four treaties signed by the president of the United States, going back forty years, and the last fifty-three each takes away more Indian land and gives nothing in return. Stop. The Blackfeet want the boundaries of their lands back where they were in the first treaty. Stop. They've got two tons of gold sitting outside in a wagon and about a thousand tons stashed in the mountains. Stop. If you guys do not change those boundaries back today to where they should be, they're going to buy every newspaper on the east coast and tell the whole story to the world. Stop. That ought to make pretty good fodder for the next election. Stop. What do you say? Do you give them back what you stole from them or do these Indians tell the world what a bunch of highbinders you are? Stop. Signed, Abraham Isaacson, Royal Maccabee. Stop."

Josh ballooned his cheeks out and blew air, then settled to his key and the tapping commenced. He finished and a few minutes later his receiver began to rattle and Josh translated rapidly. "Who is the Blackfoot leader?"

Doyle spoke to Josh. "Tell 'em Shaman."

Josh tapped it out and the next message came back. "How much gold did you say?"

"Two tons in a wagon, a thousand in the mountains," Doyle said, and Josh tapped.

"Confirm the gold," came the reply.

Doyle turned to Pat. "You tell 'em you're the law out here, and you've seen that gold, and it's real."

Pat nodded; Josh tapped; the reply came back.

"Who is Abraham Isaacson, Royal Maccabee?"

Doyle considered for a moment. "He's the founder of the Royal Maccabees Rocky Mountain Salvation Company."

Josh tapped and the reply came back. "A minister?"

Doyle grinned. "A representative of the Great Spirit."

Josh tapped and the reply was immediate. "Are you joking?"

Shaman spoke up. "No. Isaacson sent by Great Spirit."

Josh tapped, signed Shaman's name, and waited.

"Cannot change boundaries of land without Congressional approval."

"Horse biscuits," Doyle snorted. "Tell him Congress already approved those boundaries forty years ago. Everything they did since then to shrink 'em was illegal. You restore those lands today or we start buying newspapers tomorrow."

Josh shrugged and tapped. "Horse biscuits . . ."

The reply came back. "Which treaty do you mean?"

"Tell that clown it's the one with the earliest date. Tell him it's page one. Tell him he can use that treaty but change the date to today, and agree it lasts forever, and we'll forget the whole thing."

Josh tapped and then listened. "He says there's two towns now inside those geographic borders. He can't give the Blackfeet those towns."

"Fine," Doyle said. "Tell him we'll give him the two tons of gold and he can buy out the towns."

Josh tapped and the reply came. "He says all right."

"Okay. Tell him to send a copy of the new treaty over the telegraph right now. We'll receive it. Shaman will approve it so everybody's bound, and we'll exchange signed copies through the mail. Tell him."

Again Josh tapped, and there was a long pause before the receiver began to rattle.

A slow smile spread over Josh's face, and he raised his eyes to the crowd. "Here she comes. We got us a deal."

Cheering and backslapping broke out. When the receiver stopped clacking, Josh handed the treaty to Doyle, who read it to himself, then read it to Shaman.

Doyle said, "You got your land back. All of it, clear back forty years. Do you agree? Do you understand?"

Shaman nodded and clasped Doyle's hand. "Agree. Understand."

Josh tapped again for a minute, listened while his receiver rattled, and spoke once more to Doyle. "It's a done deal. They'll have a U.S. marshall here on the train tomorrow from Salt Lake to pick up the gold. And the guy with Indian Affairs will be on the train in four days with a government copy of the treaty signed by the president."

"We'll have the gold waiting," Doyle said. He turned to Shaman. "Here's a copy of the treaty. The signed one will be here in four days. Keep care of this."

Shaman took the paper and raised his eyes to Doyle's and gazed for long seconds. "Isaacson first white man keep word."

"Hold on," Doyle exclaimed. "I came out there to steal all your gold. I meant to rob you."

Shaman shook his head. "But Isaacson keep word."

Doyle looked at the old man and said nothing.

"Shaman grateful. Blackfeet grateful. You ask favor, we give favor. You want know where gold nuggets found, I tell you."

Doyle's eyes narowed. "Shaman, you promise me one thing. No matter what happens, don't ever tell me where those nuggets are. Do you promise?"

Shaman looked at him long and hard. "Shaman promise. Isaacson wise."

"Isaacson *not* wise. Isaacson not trust Isaacson," Doyle said.

For the first time since they met, Shaman smiled. "Shaman trust Isaacson."

Doyle stared at the floorboards for a moment, then raised his eyes. "Can Lump stay tonight to watch the gold?"

"Lump stay. We all stay. Shaman talk with Isaacson later."

"Okay." Doyle turned back to Josh. "Make copies of all those telegrams and give them to Pat."

He turned to Pat. "Keep those copies for the next election. You helped make a historic treaty between the president of the United States and the Blackfoot nation. You still thinking about running for governor?"

Pat looked proud. "Won't let go of me. Gompers for Governor. Got a good ring to it."

Doyle continued. "We'll help you unload that gold at the bank, and Lump will sleep in front of the vault tonight."

"I'll stay with him," Pat grinned.

Doyle raised one eyebrow. "Outside the vault, Pat."

Pat looked insulted. "Are you insinuatin' . . ."

"We're going to count those nuggets into the vault, and back out when the marshall gets here. One turns up missing, we tell Lump to find it."

Pat grimaced in disgust.

Doyle turned to Wong. "Well, we didn't get you a laundry in San Francisco."

"Wong no want San Francisco laundry."

Fan bowed before she spoke. "Ping Fat, Fan, have laundry."

Wong's eyes widened in surprise before he looked frightened.

Reverend stepped forward, his face covered with dry, flaking lather from Sven's Tonsorial Parlor.

"Did I see Maccabee on the wagon outside?"

"Yeah," Doyle said. "What's a Maccabee, anyway?"

Reverend closed his eyes to think. "Jewish warriors from the Old Testament, before Jesus was born."

Doyle shrugged. "Any of them Old Testament Jewish warriors come from Ireland?"

"Oh, mercy me no," the reverend exclaimed.

"Well, this one did," Doyle replied. He stopped for a moment to reflect. "I guess that about finishes it. I better get on down to the hotel and rent a room for the night. I'll be leaving after the marshall gets the gold tomorrow."

Shaman grasped his arm. "Shaman talk with Isaacson."

They walked out into the street as the crowd broke up and drifted back to their shops and work. Molly stayed beside Doyle.

Shaman spoke soberly. "Isaacson come with Blackfeet. We build Isaacson home. Church. School. Anything Isaacson say. Shaman old. Isaacson be medicine man."

Doyle's mouth dropped open in shock. He

clacked it shut and tried to speak. He cleared his throat and tried again. "I'm no Indian. I can't lead the Blackfeet."

"Make you blood brother. Ceremony easy. Ceremonial wine."

"I don't know anything about Indians. I wouldn't know what to do."

"Isaacson know white man. Shaman not know white man, lose land fifty-three times. Isaacson get all back in one day. We teach Isaacson about Indian. More important know white man."

Molly's eyes were bright.

"Shaman, I'm a drifter. I'm a swindler. I tried to get all your gold."

Shaman shook his head. "Doyle swindler. *Isaacson* sent by Great Spirit."

Doyle stopped cold in his tracks.

Molly seized his arm. "Tim, don't you see what he's offering? A home. A school, a hospital, a church, a chance to do wonderful things for his people. No white man ever had an opportunity like this one. Take it, Tim. Take it!"

He turned to Molly. "Me? Off over in those mountains with a tribe of Indians? You're crazy!"

"You wouldn't always be there. You'll have to travel to buy the things for the school and the church and the hospital. You'll have to find architects, and there's roads to be built, and doctors and teachers to be hired. Oh Tim, can't you see it?'

"I don't know anything about building schools and churches."

"You just forced the president of the United States to give two million acres back to the Blackfeet

Indians, and you did it in less than an hour! You were marvelous! You can do anything you set your mind to."

"Molly, I'm a con man."

"Doyle was. Isaacson isn't. Isaacson keeps his word."

Doyle took half a step backwards. "Now Molly, you can't do this to me!"

Shaman interrupted. "Shaman talk with Isaacson tomorrow."

By the time the men in town unloaded the gold into the bank vault, and Sven finished the reverend's shave, and Doyle got his room for the night, and Pat presided at the evening back room poker game, the town lights were mostly out, except for the hotel, the saloon, and Pat's back room.

Doyle walked from the hotel lobby into the soft, cool air and glanced up at the waning moon, still nearly full. He shoved his hands in his pockets and stood for a time, looking at the silvery shapes of the town, softened and nearly beautiful in the moonlight. A gentle breeze stirred up Main Street, then died. Doyle stepped into the dusty ruts and walked west, towards the telegraph office with the train station and the livery barn opposite.

A home. Church, school, hospital, roads, travel—and unlimited gold. Someone could do a lot of good with all that. Someone could help those people survive.

He watched the back room at Pat's go dark. The front door opened and the four men went their ways. Pat counted his twenty percent and pocketed it as he walked over to the bank to stay with Lump.

Doyle continued his quiet walk. *A Blackfoot medicine man. Me? That's crazy. Maccabee. An Irish Maccabee.* He smiled at the thought.

He heard the rustle at the same moment he saw the movement. He turned, feet spread, ready, balanced.

"Tim, it's me."

Doyle looked disgusted. "Molly, I told you before. People been hurt making moves like that."

She grasped his arm. "I don't know what you told those people, but Shaman is certain the Great Spirit sent you. He knows what you were, but he insists that man is gone. You're Isaacson. You have the power."

Doyle began to protest but Molly clapped her hand over his mouth.

"Maybe the Great Spirit did send you. It's possible."

He moved her hand. "The Great Spirit doesn't send con men to be ministers."

"He didn't send a con man. He sent Isaacson."

"It won't work."

"It can."

Doyle shook his head and Molly grasped his hands in hers. "Tim, I'm going with you."

She tilted her face up to his and he stared down at her.

"Molly, I told you before, it isn't fair when you do this."

"We're going," she said, and Doyle felt her arms slip about his neck.

About the Author

Ron Carter is a research and writing director for the Superior Court System of Los Angeles County, California. He received a bachelor's degree in industrial management from Brigham Young University and a juris doctor degree from the law schools at George Washington University and the University of Utah. He is the author of *Prelude to Glory, Volume 1: Our Sacred Honor; The Trial of Mary Lou;* and *The Blackfoot Moonshine Rebellion of 1892.*